"He isn't wo

Gail lay staring
"*What* did you s
him aside, but h
her waist. She was unnervingly aware of him.
"Are you *daring* to accuse me of...of——?"

"'Doing something silly' is the usual
description."

"If," she said, seething, "you have the
infernal gall to suggest I'd end it all just because
of a man—*any* man—you need your
head examined!"

Dear Reader

Over the past year, along with our usual wide variety of exciting romances, you will, we hope, have been enjoying a romantic journey around Europe with our Euromance series. From this month, you'll be able to have double the fun and double the passion, as there will now be two Euromance books each month—one set in one of your favourite European countries, and one on a fascinating European island. Remember to pack your passport!

The Editor

Lucy Gordon is English but is married to a Venetian. They met in Venice, fell in love the first evening and got engaged two days later. After fifteen years they're still happily married. For twelve years Lucy was a writer on a women's magazine; she interviewed many of the world's most interesting men. She has also camped out with lions in Africa and has had many other unusual experiences, which at times provide the backgrounds for her books.

A TRUE MARRIAGE

BY

LUCY GORDON

MILLS & BOON LIMITED
ETON HOUSE,   18-24 PARADISE ROAD
RICHMOND,   SURREY   TW9 1SR

Original edition published in 1989
by Silhouette Romances

First published in Great Britain 1993
by Mills & Boon Limited

© Lucy Gordon 1989

Australian copyright 1993
Philippine copyright 1993
This edition 1993

ISBN 0 263 78229 8

Set in Times Roman 10 on 12 pt.
01-9309-56491 C

Made and printed in Great Britain

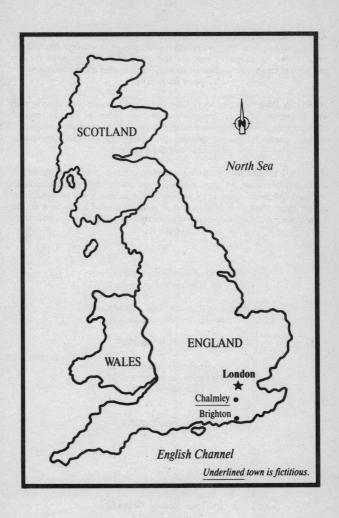

SCOTLAND

North Sea

ENGLAND

WALES

London
★
Chalmley ●
Brighton ●

English Channel

Underlined town is fictitious.

CHAPTER ONE

THE man at the corner table of the restaurant was stirring his coffee abstractedly. Gail Lawson had a sideways view that showed her the uncompromising line of his chin, the dominant nose and eyes that were deep set and dark brown like his hair. She wished she could get a better look at his mouth.

"Gail," her fiancé said impatiently, "could I have your attention?"

"Sorry," she said hastily. She lowered her voice to add, "I was looking at the man at the next table."

Harry raised his eyebrows. "Personally or professionally?"

"Professionally, of course." She smiled and added theatrically, "You know my heart belongs to you."

"Hmm. I've always felt your heart belonged to Drake Domino." He said this with the complacency of a young man who knew he was handsome. Harry had the superficial good nature of one to whom life had been kind.

Gail sighed. "Drake Domino has disappointed me lately. I thought he was going to make my fortune, but the sales of the first two books haven't been exceptional."

"But your publisher has commissioned a third book, hasn't he?"

"Yes. Dan says the readers need time to get to know Drake and I may have to write at least three books about him before the first one starts selling. At least I'm grateful for a publisher with faith in me. It's finding time to write that's the problem.''

''I thought you had all day to write. That's why you didn't take a job.''

''I don't have a nine-to-five job, but I have to earn a living. My free-lance proofreading and the odd stint for the local paper barely keep the wolf from the door, but they take up an awful lot of time.'' She laughed at herself and observed ironically, ''What I need is a sinecure with an enormous salary and no duties.''

''Why not take a proper job?'' Harry suggested. ''You can write in the evenings.''

Gail suppressed her annoyance at the suggestion that writing wasn't a ''proper'' job. It was a subject she and Harry didn't see eye to eye about, which was true of a lot of subjects, she realised. Harry was a delightful man, of course, but he couldn't understand the inner vision that made Drake Domino almost as real to her as Harry himself.

Lord Mandrake Domino was an amateur detective, not a modern private eye who slammed his opponents with a machine gun or laser beam, but an Edwardian aristocrat who dispatched his foes with a swordstick between tossing off epigrams. At other times he devoted himself to his string of racehorses and hobnobbed with royalty. He might seem an unlikely sleuth to capture public attention in the last quarter of the twentieth century, but his glittering personality fascinated Gail and, luckily, her publisher. ''The public wants a change from mindless violence,'' Dan Protheroe had said. ''Gentlemanly elegance is due to come back.''

In time he could be right. But for the moment Drake Domino couldn't pay Gail's gas bill.

"If only I could just finish the third book." She sighed now. "Then I might have the breakthrough and—" She looked up in time to catch the telltale glassiness in Harry's eyes. "Sorry," she said hastily.

He poured her some wine and summoned the waiter to order a fresh bottle. Gail looked around at the luxurious restaurant, wondering why Harry had insisted on bringing her here tonight. The palatial surroundings made her guiltily aware that they should be saving every penny for their future. "What's the matter?" he demanded.

"Nothing, it's just that—darling, I don't want to sound boring, but should we be so immoderate?"

"I like bringing you to decent places," he protested quickly. "You're so lovely, you should have only the best."

"That's sweet of you but—"

"There isn't a woman here tonight who can hold a candle to you," he hurried on. "Look." He indicated the large wall mirror behind him. The glass threw back the reflection of a young woman in her early twenties, with fair hair, deep blue eyes and a slim figure. She was certainly attractive, but to suggest she outshone every other female was going too far. But she knew Harry had paid her the compliment to silence her about his extravagance.

As she was about to look away from the glass, she saw the reflection of the man at the next table. Now she could see that his face was lean, with high cheekbones and a firm, shapely mouth that would have been attractive if it hadn't been tense. His eyes were hard and alert, and she had a feeling he was holding himself poised for action. Something drew her to meet his gaze in the mirror, and she saw that he was regarding her with an expression of cool amusement that was disconcerting. She looked away, but he remained imprinted on her inner sight.

"We talked about this before," she reminded Harry, "and we agreed not to spend so much."

"Why shouldn't we enjoy ourselves if we want to?" he demanded with a touch of belligerence.

"Because we're saving to get married. Our wedding is only a couple of months away, and you're spending money faster than it's being made."

"All right, so I spend money sometimes. But it's me that makes it, isn't it?" Harry said petulantly. "Let's face it, if you'd take a proper job, our savings would grow a lot faster."

This was unjust, because despite her lack of steady income Gail contributed to their savings steadily. She was about to point this out when she happened to glance in the mirror again and saw that the stranger was listening to them with an expression of derision that almost verged on cruelty.

Before she had time to feel indignant a wave of excitement surged up in her and she gasped quickly and began scrambling eagerly through her bag. "What's the matter?" Harry demanded as she pulled out a notebook and pencil.

Gail lowered her voice to reply, "The man next to us—he's Professor Savernake."

She uttered the last words impressively, but Harry only said blankly, "You mean you know him?"

She sighed. "If you'd ever listened to me you'd know that Professor Savernake is the evil genius whom Drake Domino has sworn to destroy. That man is just right— all dark and saturnine. He even acts strange."

"He looks normal enough to me."

"He paid for his meal half an hour ago, and since then he's sat there drinking coffee and paying for each cup separately. In spy stories that's what people do when they may have to leave suddenly."

She scribbled for a few minutes, seeking to capture her impression of the sinister stranger, then put her notebook away with a sigh of relief. Harry was scowling. "Now, if I can have your attention," he said, "I want to tell you something. A friend of mine has a boat. He's going cruising in the Aegean in a few weeks and...well...he's asked me to go, too. I'd just have to pay a few expenses, not much—"

"But what about our wedding?" Gail asked incredulously.

"The world won't end if we put it off until autumn. Come on, darling, you won't begrudge me a bit of fun, would you?" His face brightened suddenly as an idea struck him. "And you'll benefit. You can write in peace without having me in the way."

"I don't want to put off our marriage for a reason like that," Gail said, looking at him curiously. "Harry, we've been engaged for over a year, and this is the second time you've postponed the wedding. I'd gladly have lived in a rented flat, but you said we should wait until we'd saved some money for a house. But we're never going to because you keep finding other things to spend it on."

He looked around uneasily. "Hush, there are people listening."

Now she saw why Harry had brought her to a crowded place. He didn't want her to make a scene. "The trip's all settled, isn't it?" she asked bitterly. "You decided without even asking me."

He shrugged. "Come on, darling...."

Suddenly it occurred to her how often he used that phrase, usually with a shrug and a helpless look that she'd once found endearing. But what she'd fallen for when she was a naïve seventeen-year-old gave her a pang of dismay now. "Suppose I say I don't want you to go?" she asked quietly. "Suppose I want to stick to the date we agreed on?"

"We hadn't actually agreed—"

"We'd got it pencilled in." She took hold of his hand, and said urgently, "Either you want to marry me or you don't."

"Of course, I do. You know I'm crazy about you— just think of all the good times we've had together."

"But good times aren't enough. I want to be your wife and have a proper life with you, a real, solid life—"

His laugh effectively cut her off. "To hear you talking about being real and solid. You're the one who lives in a dream world."

Harry's elusiveness made her feel sick, as if she was trying to seize a shadow. She made one last try. "You know what I mean by reality. I mean being together, sharing our problems, having children—"

She felt him flinch and released his hand at once. "In other words the whole nappies-and-mortgage bit," he said. "All right, darling, all *right*. But not yet, okay?"

"So when?" she asked with a touch of anger. "When you've finished having 'a bit of fun'?"

"What's wrong with that?"

"Nothing, if you're honest about it. But you weren't. If you felt like this, why did you ever ask me to marry you?"

"Because I didn't want to let you slip through my fingers," he retorted, goaded to the point of honesty.

Gail's temper was beginning to simmer, but she spoke with deceptive calm. "In other words, you only got engaged so that you could file me away in case of future need."

"Oh, come on, dar—" Harry broke off hastily at the glitter in her eyes.

Gail felt as though she'd just seen him for the first time. Oddities in his behaviour that had puzzled her now rushed together and made sense, giving her a curious feeling of inevitability. With her attention fixed on Harry, she didn't notice the man at the next table pay for his final coffee and start to gather his things together. "I *do* want to marry you," Harry said placatingly. "I just want to live a bit first, that's all." He gave her his most winning smile. "Surely it's wiser for me to get it out of my system before we finally marry."

"*Before we finally*— Are you really so conceited that you think I'm going to wait around for you?" Her temper stopped simmering and rose to the boil. She pulled off her engagement ring and placed it on the table between them. "You can get a refund on that," she said bitterly. "The money will come in useful on your cruise."

"Hey, don't be—"

"Harry, listen carefully and watch my lips, because I'm only going to say this once. Marry you? I'd sooner marry the first man I bump into."

She gathered up her bag and rose to her feet, swinging around so abruptly that she cannoned into "Professor Savernake." He steadied her against his tall body and in that brief moment of contact she was aware of the power vibrating through him and into herself with almost shocking force. She glanced up sharply to find his dark eyes fixed on her and his marvellously shaped mouth too close for comfort. "I'm sorry—excuse me," she said tensely, and hurried away.

Outside, the light was fading. Gail began to walk with strong, vigorous steps. She'd gone a mile before she allowed herself to think seriously, and as she considered what she'd done, her footsteps slowed.

She knew she ought to be brokenhearted, and what surprised her was that she wasn't.

Gail and Harry had grown up two streets apart in Chalmley, a small but prosperous market town about forty miles south of London. She'd met him when she was seventeen, a lonely girl living with foster parents. They were kind people, but they'd never understood her or known how to make her feel as though she belonged.

But from the moment she met Harry everything had seemed to fall into place. He'd been twenty-two and dazzling. Her feelings had started as a crush for the blond, broad-shouldered young god that he'd seemed, and developed into awestruck infatuation when he deigned to date her. The awe hadn't lasted, but she'd started making excuses for him. She'd seen Harry's blithe irresponsibility, but assured herself he would mature, just as she was doing. When he'd asked her to marry him last year, it had seemed that she'd been right. What she'd overlooked was the chill of selfishness that lay just below his easygoing charm. Now she'd been forcibly confronted by it. At twenty-seven, Harry was the same callow boy he'd been at twenty-two, and Gail had outgrown him. She'd only just realised it tonight.

That realisation stopped her in her tracks. She sat down on the garden wall of a house, dropped her head into her hands and tried to sort out her thoughts and feelings. Her sadness was an ache that dragged on her heart. Five years of hopes and dreams couldn't be ended without pain, but it was a pain that would strengthen, not destroy her, because it came from the end of an illusion.

And even the illusion was getting threadbare, she thought with a sigh.

She looked up and noticed a man standing at a bus stop on the far side of the road. He was very tall, and for a moment she thought it was the man from the restaurant. Then he turned slightly as he saw her watching him, and the gesture convinced her. It was ''Professor Savernake.''

But that didn't make sense. He could have caught the bus farther back. Of course, she thought, if he'd really been the evil genius of her imagination, the waiting would have been a blind to cover the fact that he was following her.

At that moment a bus appeared and drew up at the stop. When it had passed by the man was still there.

It was too soon to get excited, she told herself firmly. He was merely waiting for a different bus. A few yards ahead of her lay the gate to a large park. If she went inside, his reaction would show if her suspicions were correct.

She hurried through the gate and left the path at once, getting out of sight in a small clump of trees. Then she moved carefully around until she could see the bus stop. There was no one there.

The trees blocked her view of her pursuer, but after a moment he reappeared just inside the park gate, quite close to her. He turned, his face a mask of baffled anger, and she thought she heard him swear under his breath. He looked like a man it would be better not to tangle with.

For the first time it occurred to Gail that she'd been unwise to approach this situation purely as a novelist. It had been fascinating to become involved, but now was the time to extricate herself, and that couldn't be done by writing, "With one bound, she was free." The man was blocking her exit.

There was nothing to do but retreat farther into the gardens until she found another gate. Moving as quietly as possible, Gail began to back away until she regained the path some yards farther on. At that very moment he turned, saw her and began to hurry in her direction.

Gail started to run and heard his footsteps speed up behind her, growing closer. She went faster, but so did he. There was no longer any doubt that this sinister-looking stranger was chasing her determinedly, driving her deeper into a lonely park full of twilight shadows, where there was no one to help her.

She was running between trees now, heading for a light just ahead where she knew there was a clearing with a river running through it. Gail could hear the water bubbling over stones. A quick glance over her shoulder showed no sign of the man, although his footsteps were all too audible.

She managed a last burst of speed, and then she was in the clearing and almost at the water's edge, travelling so fast that she had to stop quickly to avoid going down the bank. The sudden halt threw her off balance. She tried to steady herself, but her foot struck a stone and the next thing she knew she was down on the ground. The force of her landing jerked her bag from her hand. She made a frantic grab for it, but to her horror it slithered away into the fast-running water.

Gail immediately flung herself down the bank, desperate to recover the bag before it was too late. She heard heavy footsteps, and the next moment her pursuer had broken from the shadow of the trees. As she jumped into the water, he came to an abrupt halt down the bank, then hurled himself bodily on top of her.

They went into the water locked in an embrace and came up together. Gail lashed out at him as hard as she could, but the water impeded her and he had one of her arms in an unbreakable grip. She managed a few telling blows with her free hand, and after trying fruitlessly to ward them off, her attacker made a swift movement, changing his hold so that he had an arm around her waist, pulling her tightly against him. It was harder now to hit him, but she continued putting up a spirited fight as he waded to the shore and dragged her out. She tried to scream, but the struggle was taking all her breath and what came out was little more than a squeak.

She recognised with despair that she was going to be defeated. His long, lean body was pure muscle, and he overcame her easily, wrestling her to the ground and holding her there while they both lay gasping.

Two pairs of eyes met, one exasperated, one angry and apprehensive. Strangely, the very beauty of his mouth accentuated the hint of the saturnine about his face. At last he spoke, and even in her extremity she recognised that his attractive bass was the voice of Professor Savernake. "What on earth possessed you to do a thing like that?" he demanded between gasps. "He isn't worth it. No man is."

For a frozen moment Gail lay staring up at him while her incredulous brain digested this. Then she said slowly and in a voice of outrage, "*What* did you just say?"

"Of all the crazy things to do just because that over-grown schoolboy let you down—"

She sat up, trying to push him aside, but he kept one arm firmly around her waist. She wished he wouldn't. She was unnervingly aware of his power encircling her. "Are you *daring* to accuse me of... of—?"

"'Doing something silly' is the usual description."

"If," she said, seething, "you have the infernal gall to suggest I'd end it all just because of a man—*any* man—you need your head examined, preferably in the conceit department."

"Just a minute—"

"Only a man would assume that a woman who'd lost her fiancé would feel she had nothing else to live for. Do I look like that kind of spineless—?" Words failed her.

"Now wait," he said in a voice of grim patience. "I appreciate that you want to deny it now, but I saw you throw yourself into the water."

Gail ground her teeth. "I jumped into the water to recover my bag, which I lost because I was running away from some maniac who was chasing me," she said, incensed. "Oh, God, my bag! Where is it now?"

She managed to wriggle away from him and slithered down to the water's edge. The man followed and stayed close by her as if ready to forestall any desperate deed. "There it is," Gail said, pointing. "It's caught in the reeds. If I can just—"

"Stay here," he said abruptly. "I'll get it."

He stripped off his coat, jumped back into the river and began to wade towards the reeds on the far side. For a moment the bag seemed to be within his grasp, but just as he reached out, the current freed it to float on until it caught in another clump. He struggled farther along and again tried to seize the bag, but once more it eluded him by a hair's breadth and was whirled away. His desperate lunge for it only took him facedown into the water. Gail watched him surface, choking and wiping his eyes, and felt that justice had been done.

He made his way to the bank and hauled himself out. "There's a fast current," he gasped. "We'll never catch up with it tonight. And we'd better get out of here quick. It's nearly closing time, and we don't want to be locked in."

"Oh, that's fantastic!" Gail snapped. "What am I supposed to do? My front-door key and my money are in that bag."

"You can come home with me."

"Thank you very much, but I don't think I want to go with you. I don't care for the way we've met," she said sarcastically.

"I only followed you because I wanted to talk to you," he growled. "It's not my fault you headed this way."

"Of course it's your fault. You were acting like Professor Sav—acting in a suspicious manner. I was trying to get away from you, and I ended up soaking wet and locked out of my own home."

"So come to my home and dry off," he said with exasperated patience. "Then I can tell you why I wanted to talk to you."

"If it's so important, tell me now."

"This is hardly the—"

"Now!" she insisted.

He sighed. "All right. I have the perfect job for you. I'm offering you that 'sinecure with an enormous salary and no duties.'" He ignored her look of outrage at his having so blatantly eavesdropped. "Now will you please come home so that I can explain without us both getting pneumonia?''

While she hesitated, a uniformed park official appeared in the distance. ''The park's about to close,'' he called. ''Everybody out, please.''

''Come on,'' the man said, seizing Gail's hand and beginning to run.

CHAPTER TWO

THE stranger turned out to live on the edge of town in a small house that surprised Gail with its cosiness. With its thatched roof and roses around the door, it might have served for a model of what an Old-World English cottage should be. Inside she found white walls decorated with hunting prints. The ceiling timbers were exposed, and the armchairs were the old-fashioned kind, designed tó be curled up in.

Gail frowned, trying to fit the man into his surroundings, and failing. She found herself drawn to his dark eyes, dark not only because nature had made them that way, but because there were shadows beneath them. They were the haunted eyes of a man who couldn't sleep. He might plausibly have stepped out of Dracula's castle, she thought, remembering his grim, silent pursuit of her, but he looked incongruous against this traditional rustic charm. "The house isn't mine," he said, catching her glance. "I needed something to rent quickly, and this—this was the only thing I could find."

At any other time the way he'd checked himself in midsentence would have aroused Gail's professional curiosity, but now she had more urgent problems. "Could we dry off before we exchange life histories?" she asked crisply.

"Sure. Wait here." He hurried upstairs, and a moment later she heard bathwater running. He called down to her, "Okay, côme up."

She found him waiting at the door to the bathroom. "This house has settled slightly on one side," he said, "so don't shut the bathroom door or you'll have to get out through the window."

"Oh, indeed!"

"Don't glare at me like that. I'll stay out of the bathroom, I promise." Then, when she didn't relax, he said, "Look, I'm in trouble. It's almost a matter of life and death, and you're the only person who can help me. The last thing I'd risk doing is offending you."

"Mr.—"

"Steven Redfern."

"Mr. Redfern," Gail said ironically, "you've given me the fright of my life, chased me through a lonely park, caused me to fall into the water and made me lose my bag. I can't tell you how relieved I am to know that you're trying not to offend me."

He grinned faintly. "I'll try not to offend you any more than I already have, Miss—"

"Lawson, Gail Lawson."

"Go and warm up, Miss Lawson, I don't want you getting sick."

"No, I might not be any use to you then," Gail observed witheringly, and went into the bathroom, remembering not to slam the door only just in time.

She heard him go downstairs and relaxed a little, although she kept her eyes on the crack as she undressed and got into the water. It was wonderfully warm, and she slid down until her shoulders were submerged. She lay there trying to decide if Professor Savernake was running true to form. He'd lured a woman to his isolated dwelling, which sounded promisingly villainous, but then he'd run her a hot bath, which didn't. But obviously that was a ruse to make her remove her clothes, and the next step would be the offer of an innocent-looking drink that would contain a mysterious potion which—*"Hey,"* she cried indignantly as the door began to open.

"It's all right," he called from outside. "I've just brought you a hot drink. I'll leave it on the edge of the tub."

He slid his hand around the door, set the mug down and withdrew. Careful perusal revealed that it was full of cocoa.

An innocent-looking drink, Gail mused.

She dipped her finger in and tasted it cautiously, but was unable to detect the narcotic that would induce a deathlike coma while Professor Savernake bore her pathetic form to a snake-infested dungeon. Disappointment warred with reassurance, and they came out even. "Is it all right?" Steve called.

"It's fine. But don't think you're going to placate me with cocoa. Who are you? You don't sound English. Your accent is Canadian or American—"

"American," he said. "I live in Boston. I'm just here for a short while."

"Do you have English relatives?"

To her surprise he hesitated before replying, "Yes—sort of."

"How can it be 'sort of'? Either you have English relatives or you haven't."

"I have relatives, and they live in England," he said gruffly. "I'll explain about that later. I'm sorry if I frightened you. I didn't mean to, but I couldn't let you escape. You're the only person who can get me out of the trouble I'm in."

"How can you know that?"

"Because I heard what you were saying to that oaf you were engaged to."

"I don't think you should call Harry an oaf," she said, illogically indignant.

"You'd have liked to call him a damned sight worse."

"That's different. I'm his fiancée—at least, I was— and calling him names is my privilege."

"Well, I suppose I should be grateful to him for acting as he did. When I heard you getting angry with him, I knew you'd been sent to me by a kindly providence."

"I was right," she said excitedly. "You *were* getting ready to leave suddenly."

"Pardon?"

"I noticed you paying for your coffees one by one, like people do in spy books."

She heard him give a short laugh. "Yes. I had finished my dinner, then realised I had nowhere I really wanted to go, so I decided to stay for a while. Then I noticed you and saw it was obvious you were going to walk out, and I couldn't risk being left behind. I didn't talk to you right outside the restaurant because I was afraid he'd follow. I kept you in sight, waiting for the right moment. But suddenly you sat down and buried your head in your hands. That made me pause because I—well, it shook me to see how unhappy you were. He isn't worth it. I know that's hard for you to understand now, but—"

"Never mind," she broke in hastily. "I wasn't trying to do away with myself."

"Of course not. The woman who gave that man his marching orders in the restaurant could never have tried to drown herself over him. But when I saw you jump into the water and remembered how unhappy you were—"

"I'm not unhappy," she said firmly.

"That's the spirit. You're the kind of person I can do business with."

Gail began to feel *he* was the kind of person she could lose her temper with. "What sort of business did you have in mind?" she asked cautiously.

"I want to hire you for six months, for which I'll pay ten thousand pounds. There'll be an option for a further six months should it prove necessary."

The soap slipped from Gail's fingers as she heard the terms. Either this man was crazy or she was hallucinating. She was about to ask for more details when it occurred to her that she could conduct this weird conversation better if she was fully dressed. She quickly got out of the bath and was towelling herself when she discovered a new problem. "I haven't any dry clothes," she called out.

"Sorry. Wait there."

"I wasn't going anywhere," she murmured sarcastically.

In a moment his hand appeared again, holding a clean pair of silk pyjamas. Gail put them on and regarded herself in the mirror with despair. The trousers were so wide in the waist that it was only by securing them with the belt of the bathrobe hanging on the door that she got them to stay up. The sleeves came right down to her fingertips, and the legs covered her feet. She managed to roll them all up to a reasonable length, but the large jacket hung on her in folds, the front plunging almost to her waist. "I need a safety pin," she called.

"Go downstairs while I find one."

Clutching the jacket around her, she looked warily out onto the landing. Steve had vanished, and the noise from a nearby room suggested that he was turning things over in a hurry. She left him to his task and went down.

The oak staircase descended directly into a large living room, which, luckily for her bare feet, was carpeted. There were two armchairs and a long sofa covered in flowered upholstery. She opened the French windows and glanced out into the garden, but it was too dark to see much. What she could make out was a small, well-tended patch that led to a gate beyond which were some trees that rustled in the wind. She shivered and drew back into the cottage.

She looked around, seeking something that would give her a clue to this extraordinary man. A small desk, bearing papers and a portable computer, stood against the wall. Gail didn't look at his papers but she felt justified in examining the titles of the books scattered over a nearby chair. They were mostly about antiques.

Steve came hurrying down. He, too, had changed and now wore a dark red robe over pyjamas. The novelist in Gail noted automatically that both the robe and the pyjamas looked like raw silk. The woman saw that with his hair slightly tousled from drying he looked younger, less fierce and more attractive than any man had the right to. "I'm sorry," he said. "I don't have any safety pins myself, and I wouldn't know where to start looking in this house. Does it matter?" He saw Gail holding the edges of the jacket together and eyeing him askance. "You have nothing to worry about, I swear it," he insisted.

"I'll know that when you tell me what you want in return for ten thousand pounds."

He smiled suddenly. "Not what you're thinking."

Something in his smile made her feel foolish. Of course, a man with that lean, muscular frame and that piratical glint in his eyes wouldn't have to obtain female company in such a way. She clutched the edges of the jacket even more firmly together, suddenly burningly aware how little she was wearing. "So what's the catch?" she asked.

"I am. You have to marry me—not for real, of course, just for a few months."

She laughed. "All right, come on. What is it really?"

"I'm serious. I've got to get an English wife in the next few days, otherwise—" He broke off and drew in his breath sharply.

"Otherwise?" Gail echoed.

"Otherwise I'll have to leave the country," he said harshly. His voice became brooding. "That's just what they want. They think it would make me give up, but I can't give up. It would be like the end of my life, *and I won't let it happen.*"

Gail stared at him, taken aback by the transformation in his face. There was a harsh bitterness there now, and he spoke as though he were looking past her to some hated enemy. She pitied whoever had crossed his will. They would be made to regret it.

"I suppose you think I'm a bit mad," he said, seeming to become aware of her again. "Well, perhaps I am, after everything that's happened. Only a madman would pick up a strange woman like this and expect her to marry him, but that's how desperate I am."

His voice had a nervous edge, and again Gail noticed how exhausted he looked. This man was almost at the end of his tether, yet strangely she found herself less apprehensive. He'd become more human.

"Suppose you tell me about it," she suggested.

"My wife died six months ago. We'd been separated for over a year. We had two children, Nell and Kevin, and when she left me she took them with her.

"She brought them to England on what was supposed to be a visit to her parents. But the next thing I knew, she'd called me to say none of them was coming back. I wasn't happy about it but I felt they needed their mother, so I settled for visiting them as often as I could. Then Barbara died in a car crash. I rushed over, meaning to take Nell and Kevin back with me, but found myself faced with a barrage of lawyers. My wife's parents don't want to give them up. The children have been made wards of court, meaning the court is their guardian and I have to have the judge's permission even to visit them. As for having them back—" Steve finished with a despairing shrug.

"I soon realised I had a hell of a job on my hands," he continued. "My parents-in-law are Sir William and Lady Kenleigh, a very shrewd couple with a lot of influence and a lawyer who knows every trick. He kept applying for the dates of hearings to be changed at the last minute. I was traveling back and forth across the Atlantic trying to attend court and run my business back home at the same time. Once I missed a hearing because my plane was delayed. It wasn't hard for the Kenleighs to persuade a judge that 'the time wasn't right' to return my children.

"It was a hopeless situation. So I put the business into the hands of my assistant and came here to give all my time to getting my kids back. I chose this cottage because it's right on the edge of the Kenleigh estate. I see the children as often as I can, but with every visit I find new difficulties put in my way. My children are being fed stories about what a monster I am, how I broke their mother's heart. If I don't get them back soon it will be too late for us to get to know each other again. And now—'' He turned away sharply.

Steve had started calmly enough, but as he talked about the separation from his children he'd been overtaken by emotion and his voice had become ragged. Gail wished she could say something, but she knew no words could comfort such pain. While she hesitated, he strode over to the desk and took out a paper that he thrust into her hand. ''Read that,'' he said curtly.

''It's a letter from the immigration office saying that your request for an extension of your stay has been refused and you must leave the country by—'' Gail's eyes widened as she saw a date only four days away.

''I told you the Kenleighs have influence,'' Steve said. ''My lawyer discovered that they have a second cousin in the immigration service. The whole old-boy network has swung into action to get me thrown out, and this time I don't think I'll be allowed back in.''

''You're probably right,'' Gail said slowly. ''The Kenleighs are very popular.''

''You know them?''

''Not personally, but I've done some free-lance reporting for the local paper, and I've seen them at agricultural shows I've covered. Lady Kenleigh usually wins prizes for her roses, and Sir William has dogs he enters in the obedience trials.''

''The epitome of old England,'' Steve observed bitterly, ''fighting off a threat from the outsider, the *alien*—which is how I'm legally defined in this country. But I'm not alien to Nell and Kevin. I'm their father, and we're going to lose each other—unless you marry me.

"My lawyer says if I have a British wife, I can stay. I'd have time to fight. When I heard you say you'd marry the first man you bumped into, it gave me an eerie feeling because just a few hours ago I'd sworn *I'd* marry the first British woman I could find." A sudden doubt crossed his face. "You are British, aren't you?"

"Yes, but don't go so fast. I must have time to—"

"Gail, there isn't any time," he said, seizing her shoulders and looking urgently into her face. "I have four days left before I lose my children forever. All you have to do is go through the ceremony, and I'll pay six months' salary in advance. If the battle's still on at the end of that time, I'll pay for another six months. You'll have nothing to do but write your book. Don't you see that we're the answer to each other's prayers? It's almost like fate."

With his dark eyes gazing hynotically into hers, Gail was on the verge of saying yes. But she drew away from him and tried to force herself to think. She had a gift for empathy that made her feel Steve's tragedy keenly, experiencing his pain as if it were her own. But it was a gift she had learned to treat with caution because it made her too easily prejudiced towards what could possibly be the wrong cause.

She thought of Sir William Kenleigh, a bluff, jovial man. His wife was more reserved, but pleasant in a dignified, gracious way. It was hard to see them as the villains in Steve's story. Perhaps if she heard their side of things it would be Steve who appeared the villain. "Steve," she said uneasily, "I can't make a decision until I know more."

"Like what? I've told you all you need to know."

"What about your wife? Why did she leave you?"

He flushed. "I can't see that that really concerns you."

"It must. I can't intervene unless I know I'm intervening on the right side."

"I haven't asked you to intervene," he said curtly.

"But you have. If I help you win this fight, that's an intervention."

His face became dark. Gail's analytical instincts, working faster than thought, told her he wasn't used to having to justify himself and regarded it as an impertinence. "All I want you to do is go through a ceremony in return for a salary," he snapped. "You have no need, and no *right*, to judge me."

In her earnestness Gail had forgotten to hold onto the edges of her jacket. All her attention was given to confronting the furious man who stood before her, telling her that his money bought him the privilege of commanding without explanation. Somewhere far back in her consciousness she thought she heard a creak, as though a gate had been opened, but she gave it no thought. "Steve, please listen to me. It's not as simple as you thi—"

The last word was smothered as Steve reached out without warning and pulled her into his arms, covering her mouth with his own. She tensed in instinctive protest but he'd completely enfolded her. Her anger was mixed with exasperation. Did he really think he had only to kiss her to bring her onto his side? He would discover he was wrong. Gail disliked high-handedness, except in the hero of her books, whose moods she could switch off at will. Unable to fight back, she settled for holding herself rigid until he got the message.

But to her dismay she felt an insidious change begin to creep over her body. She was growing warmer, melt-

ing under the most cleverly seductive kiss she'd ever
known. Until now the only man who'd taken her in his
arms was Harry, and already a treacherous little voice
was whispering that Harry's lips had never moved over
hers with such subtle, enticing movements, caressing her
into willingness but hinting thrillingly at the pleasures
of danger. This was kissing raised to the level of fine art,
excitingly persuasive, coaxing and insisting in equal
measure.

The sensation of his tongue flickering against her lips
was delicious. Pride and annoyance urged her to resist
temptation, but another instinct, older than pride and
deeper than annoyance, made her part her lips with a
little gasp and shiver pleasurably as he slid inside.

Then a sound penetrated her hazy consciousness, and
she stiffened. Steve did the same, drawing back, and she
followed his gaze to the open French doors.

There stood a woman who looked faintly familiar.
She was in late middle age, tall, spare and upright, with
a severe face and an imposing presence. Her freezing
gaze made Gail sharply aware that the overlarge pyjama top had slid down her arms, revealing her bare
shoulders and the swell of her breasts. With a sensation of shock she realised that her nipples had hard-
ened. She hauled the silk up quickly, moving away from
Steve, hoping she didn't look as self-conscious as she
felt.

"Gail," Steve said, "I'd like you to meet Lady
Kenleigh—my mother-in-law."

"How do you do?" Gail said with as much dignity as
she could muster. She offered her hand, but the older
woman ignored it, turning on her a look of such con-
tempt that Gail flinched and lifted her head defiantly.

"Good evening, Cornelia. What a pleasant surprise!" Steve said evenly. He didn't seem ruffled by the interruption, and suddenly Gail remembered the faint click she'd heard from the garden, as though someone was coming through a gate; the way he'd seized her in his arms straight afterward. With a surge of indignation she realised that Steve wasn't surprised at all. He'd known, or at least guessed, that this was going to happen, and he'd been acting a part for the benefit of whoever was coming up through the garden. She shot him a sharp look, but this wasn't the moment to speak.

Cornelia, Lady Kenleigh, spoke in a voice that fell like ice cubes. "I apologise for intruding, Steven, but there's no need for me to detain you for very long. I only came to say that it won't be possible for you to visit us tomorrow."

"I'm coming to see my children, and they'd better be there," Steve said grimly. "I've had enough of your tricks."

Lady Kenleigh smiled glacially. "You naturally think in those terms, but Nell and Kevin don't want to see you again. I've cancelled the visit because they begged me to."

"I don't believe that," Steve asserted, although Gail saw him grow a little pale.

"You'll believe what suits you, of course," his mother-in-law replied with a small, patronising smile. "You're extremely good at rewriting the facts, which is one reason Nell and Kevin are going to be protected from the strain of another visit. It confuses them to hear a version of the past that they know isn't true."

Steve's expression became ugly. "You mean a version that conflicts with the lies you've told them," he snapped.

"There's no point in discussing this further," Lady Kenleigh asserted calmly. "You're leaving in a few days, and you will not be allowed to upset those poor children before you go. Please understand that this is final."

Steve's hands clenched at his sides. "By God, it's lucky for you that you aren't a man," he said softly.

Lady Kenleigh gave a small tinkling laugh that contained no amusement. "Oh, yes, now we come to the threats. That was inevitable, wasn't it? I know how you get what you want. But not this time. I won't let you destroy my grandchildren's lives as you destroyed my daughter's."

Her eyes flickered briefly over Gail. "I don't know what he's told you, young woman, but if you've any sense you won't believe a word of it. This is a cruel man, totally ruthless and manipulative."

"But he loves his children," Gail pointed out quietly.

"Don't confuse possessiveness with love. They're not the same thing at all, as my poor Barbara discovered. Steven wants those children because they're *his*, an extension of himself, and therefore his property. And he doesn't care whom he sacrifices to get what he wants. His wife had to run away, and his children are terrified of him. Tonight they pleaded with me not to force them to see him."

"And suppose I insist on coming anyway and get the truth from them?" Steve demanded furiously.

"Thus upsetting them even more. But I suppose you wouldn't care about that," Lady Kenleigh said with something close to a sneer. "If you have one shred of real affection for Nell and Kevin, you'll leave them alone and go quietly."

She waited to see if Steve would answer this, but he only stared at her in silent hate. "Well, I think that's everything," she said. "We won't see each other again, so I'll say goodbye now." She moved towards the French doors and smiled coldly. "Goodnight, Steven. You can get back to whatever it was you were doing."

She was gone, leaving them together. Gail looked at Steve, trying to see him through her own eyes instead of from Lady Kenleigh's perspective. But the words "ruthless" and "manipulative" echoed in her head, reminding her how he'd kissed her because he'd known someone was coming.

Steve caught her glance and sighed. "I'm sorry for doing that to you," he said heavily. "I was clutching at straws."

"You heard the gate and knew someone was coming, didn't you?"

"I knew *she* was coming. She's the only person who walks in that way, as if she owned the place."

"So the performance was for her benefit. Why?"

"If we'd gotten married, she'd have done her best to prove it wasn't genuine, so I wanted to make it look real."

"Always assuming I'd said yes," Gail reminded him angrily. "You were gambling on the hope that I'd do what you asked. Obviously most people *do*."

He threw up his hands in a gesture of helplessness. It reminded her how badly he'd been hurt tonight, and her hostility died. "I'm sorry," she said gently. "I'd like to help you, but I can't interfere in this."

"Yes, you have only my word for it that I'm not the monster Cornelia pretends," he said quietly. "And I suppose you feel I've confirmed her opinion."

Gail wished she could deny it. Her heart went out to Steve, but she couldn't do what he asked and perhaps help to send two children back to a father they feared. He wasn't a monster, but he was high-handed, arrogant and intolerant of opposition. Perhaps he was also cruel.

As if he'd read her thoughts, Steve said, "It's all right, you don't have to answer that. Wait here while I put some clean sheets on my bed for you."

"There's no need, I'll sleep on the sofa."

"You can't. I need to work down here," he said, indicating the desk. "What is it? Do you feel safer near the front door? You needn't worry. I won't trouble you, I promise."

A strong and irrational indignation took hold of Gail. It was so clear that he'd only kissed her because he hoped it would further his purpose. Now that she was no more use to him she might just as well have been a block of wood. Annoyance at him warred with annoyance at herself for minding. She restored her pride by saying crisply, "Thank you. I don't mind where I sleep if I can be sure you'll keep your distance."

"My word on it."

She supposed she ought to help him make the bed but that would have meant releasing her grasp on the jacket, and she didn't dare. Her body still tingled with the imprint of his embrace, but she didn't want to be reminded of that kiss or her own reaction to it.

At last he came downstairs and told her the room was ready. He spoke without looking at her and only grunted when she wished him goodnight.

He slept in a room under the eaves, with a sloping roof and exposed timbers. The bed was narrow but looked inviting, and she realised how the events of the evening had tired her. She wondered if Steve would mind if she borrowed one of his handkerchiefs. Moving quietly, she eased open the top drawer of his bureau. Then she stopped.

The drawer was filled with photographs of two children, a wise-faced little girl and a beaming boy, a little younger. They were shown sometimes together, sometimes singly, but the same two faces were repeated over and over, as though by endlessly duplicating the image he'd vainly sought to capture the essence of the original. This, then, was Nell and Kevin, the son and daughter Steve had come to fight for.

One picture showed Steve himself with the youngsters. Kevin was still a toddler, held in his father's strong arms. Nell, sturdy and independent, stood apart, but even she clasped her father's hand. Steve was looking down tenderly at his daughter while his cheek rested against the top of his son's head. Gail pushed the picture away, feeling a curious pain that had nothing to do with Steve.

She hardly remembered her own father, who'd vanished when she was three. But she remembered Lilian, her mother, clearly, a once-happy woman destroyed by her husband's desertion, drinking too much, until the child-care department of the Local Authority had been forced to intervene. They'd been supportive, working to keep mother and child together as long as possible. Even when they'd been forced to put Gail with foster parents, she'd been able to see her mother. But one day Lilian didn't turn up, and the next day a kindly woman came to say her mother was dead.

Gail had been only eight years old, but even then she knew enough not to blame her mother. The pathetic, spirit-broken woman had been quickly forgiven. But

Gail would never forgive her father as long as she lived. Somewhere he might still be alive, but he'd never cared enough to write to ask how she was.

Now, confronted with this blazing father love, this obstinate reaffirmation of an unbreakable bond, she found herself brushing a hand across her eyes.

There was a faint film of dust on top of the bureau and the nearby shelves. It was just enough for Gail to see where these pictures had stood until a few minutes ago. Steve must have hurriedly bundled them into the drawer, too proud to reveal his feelings to a woman who'd refused to help him. The handkerchief forgotten, Gail slowly shut the drawer, feeling like an intruder. She got into bed, switched off the light and lay there, wondering what he was really like, this man who went straight for what he wanted, indifferent to everyone else's opinions, yet whose ruthless ways concealed a streak of aching tenderheartedness.

She wasn't aware of falling asleep, but she must have, because she awoke suddenly, convinced that something was wrong. She lay in silence, then heard again the noise that had disturbed her. It came from the garden outside and sounded like voices whispering frantically. Gail rose and tiptoed to the window, opening it slowly and leaning out. But the night was dark and all the downstairs lights were off. She could make out only that someone was fumbling with the latch of the French doors.

She drew back, meaning to creep downstairs and warn Steve before the burglar burst in on him. But as she reached the top step she saw him switch on the lamp below.

At the same moment the French doors were flung open. Steve rose to his feet as two small forms hurled themselves across the room into his arms, crying, *"Daddy."*

CHAPTER THREE

INSTINCTIVELY Gail stood back in the shadows as Steve's children clung to him, crying his name. She knew she ought to return to her room. She had no part of this intimate scene, but she couldn't tear her eyes away from Steve as he hugged and kissed his children. He was a different man, one whose love had made him open and defenceless. The sight caused a hard lump to form in her throat.

It was Nell who pulled away first. Her face was streaked with tears, but there was something defiant in the way she challenged her father. "Gran said you were going away without us—without even saying good-bye," she said. "But you *couldn't*."

Steve's voice wasn't very steady as he replied, "No, I couldn't—not if you want me."

"Daddy!" The word was a reproach. Nell was crying again, unable to say more. Steve pulled her close and hid his face against her.

Kevin dried his tears determinedly. "Gran said you changed your mind about coming tomorrow because you didn't want us anymore."

"Did you believe that?" Steve demanded, looking intently at his son.

"We didn't know what to believe," Nell told him huskily. "So we waited until everyone had gone to bed and slipped out so that we could come and ask you."

"That's my girl," Steve said with the ghost of a grin. "You're never short of good ideas. Listen, you two, I didn't cancel my visit tomorrow. Your grandmother did. She said you didn't want to see *me*."

The children didn't seem surprised by this. Instead, a knowing glance passed between them. It spoke worlds about the pressure to which they were being subjected. "Gran tried to make us say we didn't want you," Nell said. "When we wouldn't say it, she got cross. Then she cried and said we were heartless."

Gail made an instinctive movement of horror at Lady Kenleigh's methods. It attracted the attention of the three below, who looked up. "This is Gail," Steve said quickly. "She got locked out of her apartment so she stayed here tonight."

Gail descended the rest of the stairs to be greeted by both children. They were polite but reserved. Nell gave her a curious glance, full of a shrewdness beyond her years, then quickly turned back to her father.

"You promised to take us home," Kevin said reproachfully. "But you haven't."

"Because—just for the moment—I can't," he said carefully. "But we mustn't give up, that's the important thing. I may have to go away again, but I'll come back and go on fighting for us all to be together."

Gail saw the children relax as though his words had given them new hope, although the situation was as bleak as before. Then she realised that it wasn't his words that had reassured them, but Steve himself. These two youngsters, lost and unhappy in a strange country, separated from their father by the law and their grandparents' emotional blackmail, still had utter faith in him. He was that kind of man.

She slipped quietly into the kitchen and searched for the milk to make the children hot drinks. Her mind was in turmoil at this new development, and she needed time to think. But she found she couldn't form coherent thoughts. All she could think of was Steve, transformed by his children, his voice gentle, his eyes lit up with joy.

She worked slowly to give them time alone together, but at last the drinks were ready, and she went into the next room. There she stopped on the threshold, held by something none of the others could see. Lady Kenleigh had arrived and was standing at the open French doors, surveying the little scene, tight-lipped. Gail had a sudden sharp sense of Steve's vulnerability. He was being spied on by a woman who hated him, and he didn't know it. She wanted to shout out a warning to him, but before she could speak, Kevin pleaded, "Can't we stay with you now? I want to go home."

"And so you shall, darling," Lady Kenleigh said at once.

Her voice startled the three in each other's arms and made them look around at her. She advanced into the room, her hand held out to Kevin, "We're going home right now."

Gail wondered if she was so steeped in self-delusion that she'd really misunderstood the child. How could she miss the way he drew closer to his father? Steve tightened his arm around his son. "Let them be," he said in a harsh voice.

"You're not achieving anything by this attitude, Steven. I'm here to take the children back where they belong. At heart that's what they want, too. You heard Kevin say he wanted to go home."

"He meant his real home—with me, as you know perfectly well."

"The only thing I know," Lady Kenleigh said with maddening complacency, "is that it's way past their bedtime. Children need order in their lives, not the kind of unruly incidents that seem to occur whenever you're around.''

''I don't call it an unruly incident when my children visit me,'' Steve returned. ''I'm very glad they did.'' His eyes met hers steadily. ''We've managed to clear up some misunderstandings.''

Lady Kenleigh had the grace to redden slightly, but she was made of the stuff that had fought on the beaches, and she didn't back down. ''What I do is for their long-term benefit,'' she said stiffly. ''They'll see matters more clearly when you're gone.''

Then somebody said, ''But he isn't going.'' And as everyone turned to look at Gail, she realised it must be she who had spoken. She didn't feel in control anymore. She could sense herself responding to a fate that had been inevitable from the moment she and Steve had met. Her voice sounded strange as she added, ''Steve isn't leaving England. We're going to be married.''

Steve tensed as if not daring to believe his own ears. Lady Kenleigh's reaction was a tightening of the lips. ''You needn't hope to fool me with this nonsense, young woman. If you were going to marry him, you'd have said so when I was first here.''

''I hadn't decided then. I have now. We're getting married at once.''

She wasn't looking at Steve, but she was intensely aware of him rising to stand behind her, his hands on her shoulders. Their light pressure burned her skin through the thin silk, and it was an effort for her to stop herself from trembling. She was stepping off into the unknown, with no way of knowing how her incredible action would end and with only this stranger's hand to hold on to.

"So you can't get rid of me, Cornelia," Steve said. "I'm going to fight to the end to get my children back, and I'm not leaving this country without them."

Lady Kenleigh's eyes narrowed, and she addressed Gail. "So you're another of his victims. Don't be fooled. He's making use of you. When he's had what he wants, he'll throw you out and you'll have come by your just deserts."

"That's for me to worry about," Gail replied evenly.

Steve dropped down until his eyes were level with the children's. "You have to go back with your grandmother now," he said. "But we'll be together soon. I'm not going without you. That's a promise."

The children clung to him one last time. Lady Kenleigh looked as if she would like to pull them away, but she met Gail's eyes, and something in the look the younger woman was giving her made her pause. A message passed between them. Steve was no longer fighting alone. He'd gained an ally whose strength had yet to be tested but who might prove formidable. At that moment he happened to glance up. He looked quickly between the two women but said nothing.

At last the children released Steve and turned reluctantly to their grandmother. "I'll be over tomorrow, Cornelia," Steve said firmly. "And I don't want any more trouble from you."

Lady Kenleigh threw him an angry look, but she knew she'd lost this round. She took the children's hands and departed without another word.

Steven watched until they were out of sight, then turned to Gail, his eyes blazing with emotion. "God bless you!" he said hoarsely. "You don't know what you've—" He choked and took her in his arms, pulling her tightly against him, kissing her with a fierceness that revealed the heartfelt depths of his relief. At least that was what Gail told herself as she felt her head begin to whirl dangerously.

The tension must have affected her, too, because her pulse had speeded up until her whole body was pounding with the thrill of the battle they'd just won. Everything about him conspired to increase her excitement. His body was lean and hard, pressing intimately against hers so that she couldn't escape the awareness of his virility or the strength of his hands holding her. The very power in those large hands seemed to drain her own energy away, and an insidious weakness flooded her, robbing her of the ability to think clearly. She knew she must fight the feeling. She needed all her wits when dealing with this man. That hadn't changed merely because she was on his side now.

She forced herself to push against his chest, ignoring the treacherous voice that said his lips felt good against hers and surely one more moment could do no harm.... "We have to talk business," she said determinedly.

He looked down at her blankly, as if wondering what she was talking about. His voice sounded as edgy as she felt. "I suppose now you think even worse of me, but this wasn't like the first time, I was just grateful—" He seemed to become aware that he was still holding her and drew a deep ragged breath. "Yes, of course. Business."

He released her abruptly, strode over to the desk and sat down to write a cheque. "Here's your first six months' salary in advance, as agreed," he said, holding it out to her. "It's all right," he added as she regarded it almost incredulously, "it won't bounce. I don't ask for what I'm not prepared to pay for."

It flashed across her mind that perhaps this was the clue to why his wife had left him, but she only murmured ironically, "You must be a millionaire."

"I am—in pounds sterling. So you have nothing to worry about."

"Look, I'm not—"

"No, you have the right to know if I can fulfil my obligations. The most successful deals are struck between people who have confidence in each other."

"In that case, you're quite right," Gail said, deciding that if he wanted to play it this way there was no point in arguing.

"That was one of the first things Cornelia disliked me for," Steve said.

"For having money?"

"For having made it myself. It's all right to have inherited wealth that your ancestors made by exploiting their serfs, or whatever they had in old England. That's nice and distant. But I built up my own fortune, which she thinks is rather crude."

"Does she think you exploited your serfs?" Gail enquired.

He gave a bark of laughter. "For years most of my workers had better pay and conditions than I did, and they worked shorter hours. I've built up a chain of retail stores selling unusual items from all over the world. That's how I met Barbara in the first place, when I was here on a buying trip. We were going to be two against the world, fighting to build up the business together, but then—" He checked himself abruptly. "But you don't want to know all that."

He was right, of course. This was a business relationship, nothing more. But as she made her way back to bed, Gail wished she knew more about the wife who'd started out with Steve "two against the world," and ended up leaving him.

The next morning they went to the nearest police station where, to Gail's astonished relief, they found her bag. "It was handed in a few minutes ago," the sergeant told them. "I was about to send out an alarm, but all's well that ends well."

As Gail examined the bag's contents she heard the policeman remark, "I didn't think we'd be seeing much more of you in this district, Mr. Redfern."

"If my mother-in-law told you I was going away, she was indulging in wishful thinking," Steve returned. "I'm about to visit my children, and I'll be here for several months." He took Gail's arm.

"What was that about?" she asked when they were outside.

"The last time I went to see Nell and Kevin it escalated into a scene with my parents-in-law. They called the police and tried to have me arrested for 'causing a disturbance'—one more step along the way to getting me thrown out. Luckily the police didn't fall for it. Now, the next thing is to arrange our wedding quickly—"

"The next thing," Gail said, breaking in on him indignantly, "is for me to go home and change my clothes. These are the ones I was wearing in the water last night."

"But they've dried, haven't they?" he demanded blankly.

She stared at him, both exasperated and amused. He didn't mean to be selfish. He just overlooked everything but the vital needs of the moment. "How do you arrange a quick wedding?" she asked.

He looked dismayed. "You're the one who's British. I thought you'd know."

"I've never got married on impulse before," she said ironically. "But I'll bet your lawyer knows. You can call him from my flat while I change."

When Steve saw her little basement flat, his amazement briefly overcame his good manners. "You *live* here?" he exclaimed, looking around at the two small rooms, one of which was dominated by a desk bearing a battered portable typewriter.

"When I'm writing I don't notice my surroundings," Gail said defensively. "There's a telephone somewhere." She pushed aside some books and papers that were stacked on the floor. "There it is."

She vanished into the bedroom and emerged a few minutes later in a pair of sturdy jeans and a comfortable sweater. Steve didn't hear her at first. He'd finished his call and picked up a copy of her first Drake Domino book. Peering cautiously over his shoulder Gail saw that he was looking at the fifth chapter, which opened with a description of Professor Savernake. She remembered how she'd almost told him last night how he resembled her lurid villain, but surely she'd checked herself before actually uttering the name? And he probably hadn't noticed anyway, she assured herself. But he seemed very intent on what he was reading.

"I've spoken to my lawyer," Steve said, looking up. "He asked if you'd been living here continuously for the last fifteen days."

"I've lived in Chalmley all my life."

"Then there's no problem. We can be married in a couple of days, in a church or a Register Office. I thought a civil ceremony would be most suitable, if you agree."

"Absolutely."

A silence fell between them. She had the feeling Steve wanted to say something but couldn't find the words. "We're quite clear what kind of an arrangement we're making?" he asked at last. "I won't ask anything from you except the legal fiction that will make it possible for me to stay in England. You'll have to move into the cottage, of course, or we won't be convincing, but we'll live our separate lives. It's just that—" He stopped.

"Steve," Gail said gently, "what are you trying to say?"

"Will you come with me today and see the children?" he asked with a touch of desperation.

"Of course, I will, if you wish."

"I'll feel safer if you're there," he added simply. When Gail's face showed her surprise that this big, confident man should feel he needed her protection, he tried to explain. "Cornelia's on her own ground, dealing with people of her own kind. When she walks into a room I can see centuries of historic tradition walk in with her and I start feeling 'alien'—and scared. So I get angry, she becomes even loftier, and I lose my temper completely."

"Thus playing right into her hands," Gail observed sympathetically.

"Exactly. But last night you stopped her dead in her tracks just by looking at her. Maybe it's because you're English, too, or maybe it's because you're a woman. Whichever it is, I saw her face. She knew she'd met her match." He touched Gail's hand briefly. "You don't know how glad I am to have you on my side."

Gail gave his hand a small squeeze but said nothing. There was suddenly nothing to say.

She'd never seen Kenleigh Grange before, but she'd heard of it as a showplace, and as they drove up the long sweeping drive, Gail could understand why it bothered Steve. It was a mansion, set in its own grounds. Since the first building in the early sixteenth century the house had been extended by extra wings and now contained Tudor, Georgian and Victorian architecture. If the blend of styles wasn't always happy, the worst clashes were veiled by the ivy that had grown over the centuries. The impression was of a grand structure that had withstood the storms of time and enemies and was girded to withstand more.

They were shown into the library and left alone. Steve stared moodily out of the French doors onto the lawns and neat flower beds. Gail studied her surroundings, which looked as if they probably hadn't changed much for a hundred years. There were the walls lined with leather-bound books right up to the ceiling, the old pictures, the shabbily grand carpets on polished oak floors. She drew in her breath in sudden excitement. This library was made for intrigue. If she half closed her eyes she could see Drake Domino unfold his long limbs from the leather sofa and go to lounge gracefully against the Adam fireplace. He was waiting for that archfiend, Professor Savernake, who would arrive through the wall, for, of course, one of those bookcases revolved to reveal a secret passage which—

Her reverie stopped abruptly as her eyes fell on something that looked strangely out of place among the faded elegance. In one corner of the room there were no books but only a profusion of horse trophies. Rosettes hung on the walls, polished silver cups adorned shelves. Moving closer she could see that the trophies had all been awarded to Barbara Kenleigh.

There were photographs, too, showing a little girl in riding clothes. She couldn't have been more than six in the first, then they ranged upward, showing her at every age into her late teens, always with horses. She had a fresh, country face, open and without guile, the face of someone who always said and did exactly what came into her head without thought to the consequences. She looked spoiled but charming, headstrong but honest.

In the centre was another photograph taken much later than the others. It showed Barbara as she must have been at the end of her life. The face had softened a little and acquired a slightly puzzled expression, as though she couldn't understand how life had gone wrong. But she was still basically the same person she'd been at twenty. Now she was dead, and her parents had set up this shrine to her where everyone could see.

Gail turned to find Steve watching. "She was horse mad," he said.

Before Gail could ask him about her, the heavy oak door opened and Sir William and Lady Kenleigh entered, followed by a middle-aged man with a bland manner and a smile that didn't reach his eyes. "I might have expected you," Steve exclaimed in disgust. "Gail, this is Thomas Brace, the Kenleighs' lawyer, whose job it is to think up ever more excuses for keeping me out of my children's lives."

Mr. Brace's smile never wavered. "It suits you to put it that way, Mr. Redfern, but you know quite well that my clients are concerned only for the welfare of their grandchildren—"

"Of *my* children," Steve snapped.

Gail glanced at him in dismay. If his fuse was as short as this, he was making it easy for his opponents. "Let's not go into that now," she put in. She was quickly sizing up the Kenleighs, noticing that Sir William looked slightly uncomfortable and had positioned himself a little behind and apart from his wife, as if to say that nothing she did was his fault.

Mr. Brace cleared his throat. "My clients have asked me to say that they are not deceived by your last-minute acquisition of a convenient fiancée nor do they intend to be intimidated into allowing matters to go further."

"It's not a question of being intimidated but of obeying the law," Gail interrupted smoothly, in a manner that was an echo of his own. "The court has allowed Mr. Redfern visiting rights that you are not entitled to obstruct, and once the wedding has taken place the law will permit him to remain in this country. As a lawyer, Mr. Brace, you must be quite aware of the position."

He fixed her with a lofty gaze. "I don't need instruction in my duty—"

"I think you do," Gail interrupted him again. "A lawyer who was doing his duty would never have stood idly by while Lady Kenleigh behaved as improperly as she did last night. Oh, didn't you know the details?" She'd caught the puzzled look he'd flashed at the older woman. "You must ask her about it when we've gone."

Gail was full of angry pleasure at the sight of their infuriated faces. These people had played a mean game, counting on Steve's hot temper to give them easy victories. But no longer. She could stay cool because she wasn't emotionally involved.

Mr. Brace wisely decided not to answer Gail's accusation directly. "Sir William and Lady Kenleigh believe your proposed marriage to be a fraud, having no validity and therefore making no change in Mr. Redfern's legal status. They intend to seek a court ruling to that effect.''

Gail could feel Steve flinch beside her and knew he'd clenched his hands. His eyes had the same black glitter she'd seen last night, and she guessed an explosion was imminent. Quickly she moved closer and touched his fingers lightly with her own. ''You can put all that in writing to Mr. Redfern's lawyer,'' she informed Mr. Brace crisply.

''And now get my children,'' Steve ordered.

Mr. Brace began, ''Surely it would be better if today—''

''*Get them!*'' Steve shouted, taking an ominous step forward.

Mr. Brace, no hero, took a half step back and collided with a chair. He stumbled only slightly, but at once Lady Kenleigh hurried forward, clucking commiseration, murmuring about ''threats and violence.'' The lawyer smiled glassily and thanked her, but Gail could see he wasn't pleased to have attention drawn to his feeble behaviour. He looked daggers at Steve. ''You'd better send the children in,'' he muttered, and left the room hastily with Lady Kenleigh.

An awkward silence fell, until Sir William asked where he'd seen Gail before. She reminded him that they'd met briefly at the last county agricultural show, and the two of them discussed farming with great determination for the next few minutes.

At last Nell and Kevin appeared, accompanied by their grandmother, and ran to Steve, who dropped to one knee to put his arms around them. Reluctantly

Lady Kenleigh allowed herself to be ushered out again by her husband. Gail went, also, and as soon as they were outside the older woman turned on her. "You see the kind of man you're getting involved with?" she demanded. "Threats and violence are the only things he knows, as you'll discover the first time you cross him. Or is he paying you enough for you *not* to cross him?"

Mr. Brace, who'd remained in the hall, made an uneasy movement and laid a restraining hand on Lady Kenleigh's arm. She threw it off impatiently. "No, I'll say what I think. Listen, young woman, I know you've been bought, and that means you can be bought again. Back out of this so-called marriage and I'll top whatever he's paying you."

In the tense silence that followed, Gail could hear Sir William holding his breath and Mr. Brace calculating the damages from a slander suit. She smiled. "I'm going to forget you ever said that, Lady Kenleigh." She moved away before there could be any answer and went quickly out into the grounds.

The house oppressed her. It sheltered too many conflicting emotions. It had seemed so easy last night to give Steve her help, but she'd acted without thinking everything through. Now she knew she had a tough fight on her hands. But at least she was sure she was fighting on the right side. The way Nell and Kevin clung to Steve told its own story.

She'd wandered part of the way down the drive, too sunk in thought to look where she was going. Now a sudden sharp noise made her glance up to see a man standing at the wrought-iron gates that led to the road. He was calling her and beckoning. Her eyes opened wide, and she gave a little gasp of dismay as she saw who it was.

"Harry."

She ran the rest of the way to stop him coming in. As soon as she reached him, Harry seized her in his arms and pulled her tight. "Darling," he said, a little too emotionally, "just tell me you're all right."

"Of course I'm all right," she said, disengaging herself and hoping no one could see her from the house. "Harry, what are you doing here?"

"Ron Sedgewick called me when they found your bag in the water."

Gail groaned. Ron was a young policeman that Harry occasionally met for a drink. She'd recently spent an evening with them. "He works at the station where your bag was handed in," Harry told her. "When he saw your papers he called me. I dashed over, and the sergeant told me where you were." His clasp on her hands tightened. "You'll never know what I've been through, how I felt when I heard your bag had been fished out of the water. Darling Gail, tell me it was an accident."

Her lips twitched. "Of course, it was an accident," she said. "What else could it possibly have been?"

"Well, I...you were rather upset when we parted last night, and I wondered—"

"Upset? I was angry, not suicidal."

"And it was all my fault. How could I ever have forgiven myself if—?" He shuddered.

"Oh, I think you might have managed it somehow," Gail observed wryly.

He frowned. "Darling, I appreciate that you've been through a traumatic experience, but I think that remark is in poor taste. I've been suffering the tortures of the damned.''

And also enjoying some gratified vanity, she thought.

''Harry, please listen to me. I haven't been through a traumatic experience. Whatever was between us has been over for some time. I only realised that last night but—'' She saw him staring over her shoulder. ''What is it?''

''Funny, that looks like the fellow in the restaurant.''

Gail turned and saw that Steve had come out of the house and was looking in her direction. She quickly pushed Harry back through the gate and out of sight. ''What's he doing here?'' Harry demanded.

''I'm going to marry him.''

He stared at her. ''Oh, my God, you meant it!'' he exclaimed. ''You said you'd marry the first man you bumped into. My poor pet, you've gone addled in the head. I know you're desperate, but you mustn't do this.''

''For the last time, will you try to understand that I'm not desperate? I'm sorry, Harry, I know I ought to be brokenhearted, but I just can't manage it. Now be a dear and go away.''

She eluded his attempt to hold her and ran back through the gates. Steve's car was already moving slowly down the drive. He pulled up, and she got in. ''That was Harry,'' she said. ''He'd heard that my bag was found and came to see if I was all right.''

''Kind of him,'' Steve said noncommittally.

''Yes. Now let's go and see about the licence.''

''Seeing him hasn't made you change your mind?''

"No. I gave my word, and I stick to it," she said briefly.

He wondered if he'd only imagined that she was agitated. He wished he could banish from his mind the picture of her taking her ex-fiancé hurriedly aside, as though she were anxious to be alone with him.

Or, at least, he wished he minded less.

CHAPTER FOUR

THE wedding of Gail Lawson and Steven Redfern took place at Chalmley Town Hall two days later. One of the witnesses was a member of the staff, the other was Leonard Berrick, the groom's lawyer. Afterward the happy couple were booked into the bridal suite of a luxurious hotel in the seaside resort of Brighton. Neither the bride nor the groom had wanted it this way, but Leonard Berrick had insisted.

Gail had to pinch herself when she'd first met him a few days before the wedding. She'd expected Steve's lawyer to be like him, young, dynamic, full of energy, but Leonard appeared to be in his eighties. He was a small man with a shock of brilliant white hair. He shuffled slowly around his untidy office, apparently on the verge of collapse, and she had the uneasy feeling that his mind was wandering. "It's no good trying to do this quietly," he'd asserted. "They'll try to prove the marriage false if they can, so you've got to make sure they can't. Yes...that's it..." He became sunk in thought, and they watched him expectantly.

"You've got to have a honeymoon," he resumed after a while, "bridal suite, champagne, all the trimmings—make as much fuss as possible, d'ye see? Spare no expense!"

The last words came out with such unexpected vigour that Gail was surprised into a chuckle. The old man's twinkling eyes met hers, and suddenly she could see how shrewd and sharp they really were. But in addition to that shrewdness, Gail thought she detected the signs of an incurable romantic. "I've made the booking for you at the Hotel Imperiale in Brighton," he said conspiratorially. "It's the best place in town."

"I expect you're well acquainted with Brighton," Gail said, laughing.

"In my young days I had some wonderful times there, but one grows old." He sighed regretfully.

Steve broke in with a brusqueness that was almost rude. "Is a honeymoon really necessary?"

"You should behave as any other newly-wed couple would," Leonard said sternly, although his impish smile belied his tone. "Never forget that they're watching."

"But will they know we're going to Brighton?" Gail asked.

"I shall make it my business to ensure that they do, so you must assume there'll be eyes everywhere—in private as well as in public." As they opened the door to leave, the old man delivered a parting shot. "One very important thing, make sure the bed's convincingly rumpled in the morning. I don't care how you do it, but *do it*." With a final wink, he closed the door.

After that they had to get themselves through the outer office, where Leonard's secretary was assiduously not looking at them, and into the corridor before Gail could collapse with laughter. "It's not so damned funny," Steve growled.

"It *is*," she insisted, but dampened down her mirth when she realised he couldn't share it.

"Let's get going," he said. "We still have things to do."

He turned away without waiting for her to answer. She caught up with him, frowning. "Why are you so irritable suddenly? Is the thought of taking me to Brighton that bad?''

"I don't know what the special significance of Brighton is,'' he snapped. "Perhaps you'd be good enough to tell me.''

"Oh, that. Years ago, Brighton had a reputation as a very romantic place. I'll bet Leonard used to take flappers there for secret weekends, in the twenties.''

"So that was the joke you two were sharing,'' Steve growled. "It's not something I'd know about.''

He strode in silence. Gail sighed, blaming herself for her clumsiness. "I'm sorry, Steve. I didn't mean to make you feel alien again.'' Impulsively, she slipped a hand into his to comfort him.

He gave it a squeeze. "No, it's my fault. I'm too touchy. Try not to take any notice of my moods.'' He grinned. "You wouldn't think it to look at Leonard now, would you?''

"He's marvellous. At first I couldn't understand why you'd chosen him, but I soon realised.''

"Yes, behind that vague manner he's got a mind like a razor.'' He seemed to become aware that he was still holding her hand and released it awkwardly. "I'll see you at the town hall,'' he said.

"Yes, fine.''

"Gail—you *will* be there, won't you?''

"Of course, I will. I told you, I keep my word.''

Later that day she opened the *Chalmley Gazette* and discovered a small headline, Local Author Weds Tomorrow, followed by a paragraph about her "whirlwind romance,'' with full details of the honeymoon destination. Leonard hadn't missed a trick.

She had only a short time to buy the right clothes for a wedding and honeymoon in a luxurious hotel. The last time she'd spent real money on herself had been when she was a teenager, and she discovered she'd now acquired an elegance and poise that made her purchases all the more worthwhile.

She bought a cream jersey dress that would be ideal for the ceremony. Then her eye fell on a nightdress and peignoir set in white silk chiffon. It might have been made just to frame her fair loveliness, and she wanted it with all her heart, but the price troubled her conscience.

I'm not spending Steve's money, she argued with herself. *This is coming out of my own savings, and so is that pair of little white slippers—I mean they would if I bought them—which I'm not going to do.*

She reminded herself that Leonard had said, ''Behave as any other newly-wed couple would.'' Surely that meant dressing to look good on her ''wedding night.''

But it wouldn't mean going to a plush hotel in a blaze of publicity, she thought. *Just to get him to myself, alone somewhere, far away from the rest of the world...* She drew a deep breath at the direction her thoughts were taking and added hastily, *That's what I'd want if I were in love with him.*

She bought the lingerie and the slippers.

She arrived a few minutes early at the town hall next morning, to find Leonard and Steve waiting for her, plus a photographer from the *Gazette*. ''Leonard overdid it a bit, didn't he?'' she whispered to Steve.

''Impossible,'' Steve hissed. ''If you're going to tell a lie, make it a big one.''

The ceremony took just ten minutes, then they were on their way out again, and Gail was smiling and laughing like any other bride.

Until she saw Harry.

He came around a corner of the building just as the bridal party appeared at the top of the steps and stopped to stare at them. Gail felt a pang of sadness at the sight. Harry's face was desolate, not with disappointed love, but with the bafflement of a child who couldn't understand how this could actually happen to him.

He didn't think anything could be taken from him, even something he didn't much want, she thought.

Meaning only to be kind, she smiled and impulsively tossed him the small bouquet she was carrying. Steve scowled but didn't have the chance to say anything. Leonard kissed the bride with gusto, murmuring, "Unwise, dear lady, but no real harm done, I think."

There was no reception. The wedding had been planned early to leave time to drive to London to deal with the paperwork. Steve swung the car away from the town hall. They were well on the way to London before he spoke. "I suppose that was a pledge for the future," he said grimly.

Gail, who hadn't been thinking about Harry, was startled by his question. "What?"

"That touching little gesture with the bouquet. You're planning to marry him when you're free of me, aren't you? But I don't want him stirring up trouble by hanging around you while we're married."

Gail was so incensed by this speech that she couldn't decide which part to answer first. "You really are a charmer, aren't you?" she exclaimed scathingly at last.

"If anyone from the Kenleigh side had seen what you did, it could have been dangerous," he pointed out.

She sighed. "Yes, it could. I'm sorry. I forgot for a moment. I used to be fond of Harry, and he looked so much like a little boy lost that I just felt sorry for him."

"Don't confuse pity with love, Gail."

"I'm not likely to." Then, because she felt uncomfortable discussing Harry with Steve, she said, "I suppose you know how to find the Aliens' Registration Office when we reach London?"

"Yes, I know," he said, letting her change the subject.

At the office they showed Steve's passport and their marriage certificate. There was a long, nerve-racking moment as the official looked the two documents over, turning the pages of the passport back and forth while the two of them held their breaths. Then he grunted and stamped the passport with the word Residence.

Steve fixed his gaze on that stamp, and his face was flooded by such overwhelming, heart-wrenching relief that for a moment Gail felt her throat tighten. He took her arm and led her outside. "Thank you," he said as if in a daze. "Gail—*thank you.*"

His anguished joy invaded her, making something in her leap towards him. He moved as if to embrace her as he'd done before, and she felt her lips begin to tingle in anticipation—or was it memory? She hardly knew that she'd drawn a quick breath and leaned slightly nearer to him, but in another moment she was sure she would be in Steve's arms, feeling the force of his emotion against her willing mouth.

Then he dropped his hand from her arm and said, "It's getting late. We'd better head for Brighton."

"Yes," she said, feeling absurdly like a child that had been denied a promised treat.

He headed the car out of London towards the south coast. Gail sat in silence, trying to understand her own thoughts, but it was difficult because although she was shrewd at dissecting other people's natures her own was often a mystery to her. All she knew was that the brief moment's happiness had vanished and she was full of tension that was rising rapidly.

After a while Steve said, "Why do you keep looking out of the back of the car?"

"I want to see if anyone's following us." She sighed, adding, "but there's nothing."

"You actually sound regretful."

"I've never been pursued in a car before."

"You mean you want to be?"

"I'm a writer. It's all grist to the mill."

Steve grinned. His mood had improved. "Well, I'm sorry I can't lay on an exciting chase."

"Never mind." She yawned. "I'm tired anyway. I hate packing. I always forget things."

"You can't have forgotten anything. One of your bags weighed a ton."

"That's probably the one with my portable type-writer."

The grin was wiped from Steve's face. "What do you mean, 'portable typewriter'?" he demanded.

"You know what a portable typewriter is, surely?"

"Of course, I know what it is. What I don't know is why you brought it on our honeymoon."

"Well, I've got to do something, haven't I? How else do you expect me to pass the time? *Steve*, be careful! You nearly sent that man white-haired."

"Sorry, the wheel slipped from my hand for the moment. Gail, this is nonsense. You can't be a convincing bride if you spend all your time *typing*."

"I won't do it while anyone's there—"

"People will hear. We're in the bridal suite, for Pete's sake."

"You're right," she said. "I hadn't thought of that."

Misled by her innocent tone, he gave a sigh of relief and said, "I knew you'd be sensible."

"I'll have to buy a portable computer, they're nice and quiet. And if I get one like yours, you can show me how to work it."

He ground his teeth. "The hell I will!"

"Why be disobliging for the sake of it?"

After that, it escalated. Words were said. They reflected the strain of the situation rather than what either of them felt, but they left their mark on two people whose sense of proportion had deserted them. To cap everything, the heavens opened. "That's all it needed," Steve exclaimed in disgust. "Doesn't the weather in this country ever do anything but rain?"

"Yes," Gail informed him glacially, "sometimes it snows."

"We're going to have a great time at a seaside resort."

They got lost and arrived in Brighton late in the evening, barely on speaking terms. Steve halted the car in front of the Hotel Imperiale and got out to retrieve the luggage from the trunk. "You go in and register while I park," he said, adding, with a glance at the doorman, "darling."

An elderly woman at the reception desk looked up and smiled at Gail. "Better late than never," she said. "Was it a terrible journey?"

Gail returned pleasantries while she registered. She was longing for a meal, a bath and a good night's sleep.

"Oh, dear." The receptionist was looking at where Gail had signed. "I thought it would be Mr. and Mrs. Redfern, in the bridal suite."

"Of course," Gail said, hurriedly crossing out her maiden name. She looked up as Steve approached, then at the floor around her. "Someone's taken our bags," she exclaimed more sharply than she'd meant to.

"It's all right," he soothed. "Don't panic."

"I'm not panicking. It's just that I turned around and they'd gone—"

"Because I've just sent the porter upstairs with them. Trust me to know what I'm doing."

"I never suggested that you didn't know what you were doing. I only—"

"Ahem."

They both turned to the receptionist.

"Here's the key to the bridal suite," she said, "and you'll find a small token of the management's good wishes inside. May I wish you both a very enjoyable honeymoon and a long and happy marriage?"

"Thank you," they recited dutifully.

As Gail turned away, the receptionist laid a gentle hand on her arm. "I know just how you feel," she whispered. "People always quarrel on honeymoon. My husband wasn't even speaking to me when *we* reached the hotel." She gave a little worldly-wise nod. "But you'll feel so much happier in the morning, I promise."

It dawned on Gail that she and Steve were supposed to be suffering from frustrated desire. She had to press her lips together to control a wild impulse to laugh.

But in the same moment she stiffened as the truth burst on her. The old woman had instantly recognised the feelings Gail had denied. From the moment she'd seen Steve reflected in the restaurant mirror, he'd physically intrigued her. His kiss that night had been a revelation of how a man's body could affect a woman, how it could ravish her senses with its warm muskiness and tormenting desirability.

She'd refused to face the reality, and all the time it had been lying in wait for her. She wondered if Steve felt the same, and stole a glance at him as they rode up in the lift with the porter. But it was impossible to tell anything from his face, and all he said, was, ''I could do with a good meal.''

''You'll find the room service menu in the bridal suite, sir,'' the porter said.

The bridal suite could have been an enchanted place to a couple in love. The furnishings were traditional, centred on a huge, luxurious four-poster bed hung with crimson brocade curtains. Two tall windows led onto a balcony overlooking the sea, which murmured forlornly in the darkness. In one window enclosure was an ice bucket bearing a bottle of champagne. In the other was a large basket filled with red roses, compliments of the management.

When they were alone, they solemnly poured champagne and clinked glasses. ''Sorry, I'm such a bear,'' Steve said. ''I don't know what's gotten into me. I expect you're giving thanks you're not really tied to me for life.''

''You can be sure of that. It would be a dreadful prospect,'' Gail assured him cheerfully.

While he was calling room service, she went exploring and found that the suite had, among other things, two comfortable armchairs and a luxuriously appointed marble bathroom. But with growing dismay she realised that it didn't have a sofa long enough to stretch out on. In the rush of the last two days she'd overlooked this problem, but now it suddenly loomed large.

Despairingly she wondered why they'd ever let Leonard talk them into this ridiculous honeymoon. Even her love of the dramatic couldn't persuade her they were really being spied on, and now she'd got herself holed up for a week with a dangerously attractive man, with nothing to do but pretend to be lovers, and only one bed.

Steven had finished with room service and was calling his assistant in Boston, talking business. Gail started her unpacking. At last there came a knock on the door, and she opened it to a middle-aged waiter, who wore a name tag saying Martin. He wheeled the loaded table inside and began to set it up, performing every action very carefully. Gail wished he would be a little quicker. But perhaps he was waiting for the ''happy groom'' to come off the phone so that he could pour them some wine. His eyes had flickered to Steve several times.

And at that moment Gail felt the hairs begin to stand up on the back of her neck.

Steve hung up a few minutes later and turned to find himself alone with his bride, who'd changed into white silk chiffon lingerie that suggested almost as much as it concealed. Suddenly his throat was dry. That flimsy material, designed to disappear under a man's caresses, was clearly chosen for seduction.

But whose seduction? It was strangely important to know. Suppose this was part of a trousseau she already possessed? Had that callow oaf she so unaccountably loved—whatever she pretended to the contrary—been meant to feast his eyes on the plunging neckline and lay his face between the beauty of her round creamy breasts?

He tried to read the answer in her eyes, but failed. Of course, she was fulfilling a business contract. She'd reminded him of that in the car when she'd asked him what else there was for her to do on their honeymoon but write. The realisation of what he would have liked her to do had almost made him lose control of the car. Now he found himself giddy from the desire to accept the invitation of those seductive clothes, while she stood regarding him with unruffled coolness. Confusion made him speak shortly. "I suppose I should dress for the occasion, too. Will dinner wait for me?"

"Of course. But don't be too long," she replied brightly.

He emerged from the bathroom a few minutes later in pyjamas and robe. Gail almost wished he hadn't changed. It was hard not to look at the dark hair that came almost up to his throat, and harder still not to wonder how it would feel to trace it softly downward, letting her fingertips luxuriate in its curls. Her thoughts made her perilously aware of how thinly she was covered, and she drew the edges of the peignoir together, fearful lest her feelings should be revealed by her glowing skin.

"I agree," Steve said wryly.

She jumped. "What?"

"You were thinking the same as me, weren't you— that this is really rather ridiculous?"

"Absolutely," she said heartily. She was glad she hadn't voiced her suspicions of the waiter, which now seemed idiotic.

"Leonard let his imagination run away with him, and now we're stuck here. Never mind, we'll just have to make the best of it."

"Shall I be a good wife and serve you?" she inquired politely.

"Thank you."

That was a mistake, he realised, as soon as she leaned forward, filling his nostrils with the perfume of her body's warmth. Out of sight, he gripped the chair.

"You really went to town to get the costume right," he said, hardly knowing what he said. "I hope you didn't break the bank."

Gail looked down at the chiffon and thought of her secret pleasure as she'd tried it on, pleasure that she only now understood. But to him it was just "the costume," an item to be added to expenses. "It won't break *your* bank," she informed him coolly. "It came out of my own savings."

So she had *bought it for Harry,* he thought.

Silence.

"This steak's good," he said desperately.

"I don't know when I've tasted better."

They ate for a while.

"I'll sleep on the sofa tonight," he assured her.

"There isn't one. I've already looked."

Of course, she had. It was probably the first thing she'd checked.

"Well, I'll think of something," he said lamely. He wondered if she was looking at him but seeing Harry.

For the remainder of the meal they covered their inner dismay with a studious politeness. As they were finishing there came another knock at the door, and the waiter called, "May I collect the table, sir?"

"That's very odd," Gail said before Steve could answer.

"What is?"

She didn't answer directly but rose and went quickly to stand beside the bed, her manner full of suppressed excitement. "Come here," she urged.

Puzzled, he went to stand beside her, just as she called out, "All right, you can come in."

Several things happened then. The door opened and the waiter entered. At the same moment Gail threw her arms around Steve and pulled him down to the bed with her. Before he had time to recover from his surprise she'd moved over him, letting her hair fall into a curtain that cut them off from the outside world. He had a moment's blinding vision of her face above him, and his senses swam. Then she came closer until her lips were next to his ear and whispered, ''That waiter is a Kenleigh spy.''

She locked her mouth onto his before he could react, sliding her fingers into his hair in a skilled imitation of devouring passion. Steve knew a moment of furious disappointment that this was a performance, then indignation was swallowed up in the other sensations that were taking him over.

He could still recall how her body had felt pressed next to his on the night they met. The memory had haunted him through the last two hectic days when the whole of his attention should have been given to other things. He'd been sure he could remember every detail. Now he found he was wrong. She was a thousand times sweeter and more enticing than any memory, and he could no more have stopped himself responding than he could have flown.

Gail had meant to keep control of herself and do only what was necessary to her role, but once in Steve's arms she forgot everything except that she was yielding to her clamorous instincts. He felt good against her, and that feeling raced through her body, pervading her flesh, making it glow as never before. Her lips belonged to his. She'd known that since the first kiss, and now she wanted to explore the mouth whose mobility enchanted her and whose stillness intrigued her.

She gave herself the pleasure of exploring it thoroughly, and felt it move against hers, giving back ca-

ress for caress, answer for question. Then he moved
suddenly, rolling over until he was on top, controlling
the kiss. "Do you think this is what he wants to know?"
he whispered against her lips. Gail tried to answer but
found the sound coming out as a little gasp. He took
advantage of her parted lips to slide inside, finding her
tongue, teasing it, luxuriating in the silky inner surface
of her mouth.

Gail felt tremors go through her at that skilled as-
sault. Nothing in her life had ever excited her so much.
Hunger for him, shocking in its urgency, rose up, almost destroying the last of her control. She slid her
arms around him, letting the fingers of one hand caress the nape of his neck, while the other hand felt the
iron muscles of his back. To her infinite pleasure she
could tell that she was driving him to the brink of mad-
ness.

But there was another world beyond the brink, a
world of delight that they could explore together. She
yearned to cross that boundary with him, whatever the
risks. She wanted to wrench open his pyjama jacket and
pull him against her so that she could feel the rough hair
of his chest against her skin. She wanted to be naked
with him, free to caress him and discover him everywhere. Above all she wanted him to desire her in the
same way, and the bruising urgency of his kiss told her
that he did, that for him, too, the exciting forbidden
world beckoned.

Steve drew back from her a little and lay looking
down into her eyes. His face was suffused with passion, his eyes dark and glowing. He took a long ragged
breath and was about to speak, when the quiet sound of
the door closing made them both freeze.

That sound, with its reminder of reality, shocked them out of their dream. In a daze they pulled apart, looking at each other, alarmed and wary. They were strangers who hadn't learned to trust each other, and so, despite the revelation of passion, their eyes were veiled and defensive.

The waiter had vanished, taking with him the table. Steve got to his feet, hoping that his shaking limbs would support him. "How did you know?" he asked.

"Know what?" For a moment Gail wasn't sure what he was talking about.

"That he was a Kenleigh spy."

Gail forced her scattered wits back to some semblance of normality. "When he delivered the meal, you were on the phone and he kept looking at you," she said, getting up and fixing her peignoir firmly around her. "I wasn't sure then, but I was when he came back. They wouldn't disturb a honeymoon couple like that. They'd wait until we called or leave us to put the table outside the door."

"You've got all the details worked out," he said admiringly. "But I forgot—you're a crime writer."

Each had been waiting to see if the other would show any awareness of what had happened. Now they knew that neither would. "I think I'll wash the dirt of the road off me," Steve said, and vanished hastily into the bathroom, hoping she wouldn't comment on his lame excuse for distance. Once there, he turned the shower temperature down to freezing.

He reappeared half an hour later and stopped in the doorway, riveted by the sight of Gail jumping up and down on the bed as though on a trampoline. "Remember what Leonard said about rumpling the bed," she gasped between leaps.

"Wouldn't tomorrow have sufficed?" he protested, surveying the damage she was causing.

"I wanted to make sure—we didn't—forget," she puffed.

He grinned, his equanimity restored. "Damned if I know how I ever fell in with a wacky character like you," he said.

"A woman who'd marry the first man she bumped into would do any tomfool thing," she pointed out.

She finished her game and slithered down to a sitting position on the bed. With her flushed face and tousled hair she looked as if she'd been having fun. Steve felt an impulse to kiss her, not passionately, but with a surge of protective affection such as he might have felt for a mischievous child. He gave a sigh of relief that the danger was past.

CHAPTER FIVE

"IT LOOKS as if Leonard was right," Gail remarked over breakfast the next morning. "The hotel staff have certainly been bought."

At Gail's suggestion they were eating in the public breakfast room, "to give us a chance to study the people who are studying us."

"Brace must have got onto it damn quickly," Steve murmured. "He only had about twenty-four hours. Do you think he aimed at everybody?"

"No, just the ones who normally serve the bridal suite."

"Well, we gave the waiter plenty to tell him," he said with a wry glance at her.

She laughed. "Yes, but I think you ought to follow it up with a really huge tip, just to ensure he tells Mr. Brace what he *really* saw and not merely what he thinks is expected of him."

"Have you done this before?" Steve demanded, sounding slightly alarmed.

"No, of course not."

"Well, I'm beginning to wonder. You know some strange things."

"Think of it from the waiter's point of view. He probably doesn't earn very much. Hush, here he is now."

Martin appeared, his face covered in a professional smile, his eyes alert. "Good morning, sir, madam. I trust everything was to your satisfaction."

Steve was about to make a noncommittal reply when Gail fixed him with adoring eyes and breathed ecstatically, "Oh, yes, thank you. *Everything.*"

Steve's face was a study of surprise. Martin's expression remained carefully blank as he intoned, "I'm so glad. Shall I take your order now?"

When he'd departed, Steve asked in a furious whisper, "Was that really necessary?"

"Was it necessary to imply that you're the greatest lover of all time?" she asked innocently. "A combination of Casanova, Don Juan, Lothario—"

"Gail, if you don't cut it out...!" he growled.

She wasn't sure what devil had got into her, except that her nerves were on edge again this morning and teasing Steve was her only release. But he got his revenge a moment later, taking her hand as Martin approached and murmuring, "Sweetheart," as he brushed his lips against the palm, almost as if he didn't know he was sending waves of heat through her.

Last night they'd shared the big bridal bed and had lain for some time looking up into its brocade heights, sharply conscious of each other, not daring to move. Gail had been sure that if she talked to herself logically she could start to see things in the right way.

I'm very good at being logical, she'd reassured herself.

It was something she'd learned as a child, or perhaps it had developed out of her traumatic experiences. Her foster mother had often said, "Gail is the sensible one," looking at her in an odd way, at if to imply that she was too sensible for her age. And it was true, she'd had an unchildlike ability to step outside a situation.

In the early months of fostering, her new parents had braced themselves for tantrums and delinquent behavior, but there had been none. Gail had coped by retreating into her vivid fantasy world, a place where she could control events instead of being battered by them.

Alongside this she'd developed a gift for viewing life with a shrewd, half-humorous eye. It was balanced by a fundamental warmheartedness that prevented her from ever becoming too detached, and later she came to see it as part of a novelist's armoury. But in those days her clear, ironic mind had often made her a loner.

Last night she'd tried to make it work for her, standing back to see herself and Steve in proportion; two people feeling their way through a tense situation, with no guidelines. But the words echoed uselessly inside her head. They meant nothing beside the memory of his lips burning hers, his tongue teasing and seducing her, his aroused body pressed against her own.

At last she'd fallen into an uneasy sleep that was haunted by Steve. But somewhere in her dreams, Steve turned into Professor Savernake, and she awoke again in the early hours, possessed by a quite different kind of excitement. She slipped quietly out of bed and went into the bathroom where she could put the light on to make notes.

Now she knew what was wrong with her villain. He lacked the thrilling black magic that should make a woman find him intriguing as well as devilish. That half-acknowledged attraction to stylish anarchy was the spice that her first two books lacked. But when she wrote them, she hadn't met Professor Savernake in the flesh. For the next hour Gail forgot everything but the sheer joy of having discovered the elusive something that would make her creation work. At last she crept back to bed, noting with relief that Steve seemed as soundly asleep as before. She was sure now that she'd discovered Savernake's secret, everything would be all right in the morning.

But in the morning Steve was still Steve, and the touch of the saturnine in his dark good looks still gave her a twinge of pleasure that wouldn't be suppressed. When he brushed his lips over her palm at the breakfast table, she had to fight not to show the reaction that trembled through her. "What shall we do today, darling?" he murmured.

Gail waited until Martin was out of earshot before whispering, "Well, we could always retire to the bridal suite and put a notice on the door saying Do Not Disturb. Then you can get on with your business calls, I can work at my typewriter and the world can think what it likes."

A grin spread over his face. It was the first time she'd seen him smile without strain, and she noticed how it transformed him, revealing an unexpected charm. She forced herself to regard him with a novelist's critical eye, remembering that it was Professor Savernake's *charm* that made him so dangerous. "Nothing fazes you, does it?" Steve said with a hint of admiration. "But seriously, what shall we do?"

"I thought of taking you to see the Lanes. It's a rabbit warren of antique shops, and you're interested in antiques, aren't you?"

"I'm beginning to be nervous of those eyes of yours. They seem to see around corners."

"There's no magic in it. You had some books on antiques in the cottage."

He nodded. "My stores deal in exotic and unusual goods. I've built them up on the cheaper end of the market, but now I want to expand into something better."

It was a good morning. The sun was out, and Gail risked a blue linen summer dress. Steve was delighted with the Lanes, and they wandered the narrow, cobbled streets for hours, exploring ancient little shops that had hardly changed since the town was founded. He showed considerable knowledge and in a few hours had spent a small fortune on items for his stores. Once he glanced uneasily at Gail and muttered, "Sorry about this. You don't mind, do you?"

"Not in the least," she said, meaning it. She was fascinated by this new side of him.

Afterward they browsed in an antiquarian bookshop, and when Steve saw her gazing wistfully at an illuminated volume, he promptly bought it for her. "That's for being nice about this morning," he said. "I must have been a pain in the neck, and you were very patient."

"But I'm a paid employee," she protested. "My time is yours for the next six months."

He grimaced. "I'd forgotten."

They were just stepping out of the shop when Gail suddenly paused. Raising her voice, she cried, "Oh, darling, another wedding present. You're spoiling me."

"Oh, God, not again," Steve muttered, getting onto her wavelength at once. He slipped an arm about her shoulders and drew her close, murmuring, "Where?"

"Just over the way. That young woman in the green flowered dress. I wasn't sure until now, but she stops when we stop and goes on when we do. Quick." She seized his hand and pulled him down a side alley, then straight into another antique shop. Standing well back in the shop they were able to observe the woman hurry into the alley after them and stand baffled by their apparent disappearance.

"I don't remember her from the hotel," Steve said.

"No, I think she comes from outside. It shouldn't be hard to find out from where."

"How are you going to do that?"

"I'm going to let her tell me."

He laughed. "You'll never make her do that."

"Watch me." She left the shop, and he followed her, fascinated. The young woman fell into step behind them, looking casually about her but always keeping them in sight. After a while Gail stopped to look into a tea shop, seemed satisfied with what she saw and led the way inside.

"It's packed in there," Steve protested.

"That's why we're going in," Gail said in the voice of someone stating the obvious. After that Steve said no more.

Gail bagged them a table that was just being vacated. After a moment their pursuer entered and looked around at the crowd. Gail attracted her attention. "It's dreadful, isn't it?" she said sympathetically. "But you can share with us."

She cleared a seat where she'd dumped her bag and indicated for the woman to sit down. Before Steve's eyes she changed character, becoming gossipy and a little foolish. "I felt I had to ask you to sit with us," she confided. "You looked as if your feet hurt. I know just how that feels. My feet always hurt when I was a reporter—heavens, the miles I walked just trying to catch up with people! Are you on holiday here?"

"No, I live here," the young woman responded. "What a funny coincidence, you being a reporter."

After that it was only a matter of time before Gail knew the young woman's name, which was Clara Devon, and her occupation, which was free-lance journalist. They swapped stories of life on provincial papers, including the low pay. Gail coyly admitted that she'd actually published two books and was working on another, although, of course, she couldn't think about working just now—with an adoring glance at Steve. She offered to send Clara copies of Drake Domino's early adventures and carefully wrote down Clara's address and phone number. It was a dazzling piece of psychological conjuring, and Steve watched it in silent, delighted awe.

"You're loving this, aren't you?" he said as they made their way back to the hotel.

"I haven't enjoyed myself so much in ages," she admitted.

"How did you know she was a journalist?"

"Elementary, my dear Watson. Actually it was an educated guess. She reminded me of myself when I was doing legwork, and if Mr. Brace wanted to spy on us outside the hotel, a local free-lance in need of a little extra cash was the most likely person for him to try."

"You seem to have a gift for intrigue," he remarked drily.

"As long as I'm writing about Drake Domino, I need it. He's a sleuth who lives in a world where nothing is quite as it seems."

"I'm beginning to understand about things not being what they seem," he said, looking at her. "I know even less about you than men normally know about the women they marry. And heaven knows, that's little enough."

"I can't help it, Steve. I'm made this way. There's always a voice running through my head saying, 'Can I use this someday?'"

"Always?" he echoed, his eyes kindling.

"Pretty well always."

Their eyes met, and for a moment the shared memory of last night lay between them. Then they backed off. Neither was ready to face it yet.

They got through the week better than either of them had feared. Steve called Kenleigh Grange every evening and was allowed to speak to his children without difficulties being placed in his way. His spirits soared after these conversations. "Cornelia's beginning to see sense," he told Gail exultantly. "It may be easier than we'd hoped."

"I wonder," she mused. "Doesn't it seem a bit too easy?"

"What's that supposed to mean?"

"I'm not sure. I'm just suspicious."

"You see conspiracies everywhere," he said cheerfully. "Cornelia knows she's lost now you're on the scene. Come on, I'm going to buy you the best dinner you ever had."

Gail tried to shrug aside her little nagging doubt, but she felt he was relaxing too soon. There seemed to be a curious blind spot in Steve's make-up. He was an astute businessman who'd made a fortune out of nothing, which meant he was no pushover. But where his personal relationships were concerned his shrewdness seemed to desert him and he fell back on raw, unreasoning emotion that clouded his judgment and left him almost defenceless. It gave her a strange feeling of protectiveness towards him.

But she didn't press the point because she couldn't bear to destroy his hope and, also, because it was pleasant to dress up and let Steve entertain her. He was a seafood addict who delighted in seeking out good waterside restaurants. Gail had never tasted seafood more exotic than fish and chips before and with her first bite of oysters she thought she'd gone to heaven. Steve laughed at her blissful expression. "It's a treat to be with someone who feels about it as I do," he said. "I'd like to take you to a *real* seafood restaurant in Boston and give you Wellfleet oysters with caviare."

"Did Barbara like your American seafood?" Gail asked. She was curious about his late wife and would have liked to ask about her sooner, but she knew she had to approach the subject carefully.

Steve frowned and sat in silence so long that she was afraid she'd made a mistake, but at last he said, "I don't think Barbara liked anything about my country—including me, eventually. I didn't realise just how deep that went until I found she'd been working to turn Nell and Kevin against me. She didn't succeed. The kids and I have a bond that nothing can destroy. But she tried, and—" he paused before saying heavily "—I can't forgive her for it."

"She tried to turn them against you while you were still living together? Steve, are you sure?"

"Of course, I'm sure," he said sharply, but added at once, "I'm sorry. It's difficult for me to talk about Barbara because I know I shouldn't speak ill of the dead, but sometimes I almost hate her for what she did to me, what she's still doing."

"You once said something very revealing," Gail commented. "You said men know little about the women they marry."

"It's true, more so with Barbara and I, perhaps, than with most couples, because we were foreigners, and I suppose we found each other exotic. I was over here on a buying trip for my first store, and we met at an agricultural show where I was looking for country crafts. She was riding in the horse event, and I remember she fell and got up laughing.''

"That can't be easy to do," Gail observed. "She sounds charming."

"That's what I thought. I walked right up and introduced myself. To me that was the natural thing to do, and Barbara seemed to like it. But Cornelia looked askance because I hadn't been introduced by someone from their set. From the start she made it clear I wasn't good enough for a daughter of old England. She kept telling Barbara that I wasn't 'their kind of person.' Which meant I wasn't a stockbroker called Nigel or a banker called Cedric. Barbara used to meet me in secret because of the fights at home, and in the end we eloped.''

"How long had you know each other then?"

"Three weeks. That was all the time I had in this country."

"And you took Barbara back to Boston with you?"

"That's right. At first we didn't have much to live on because I was putting every penny into the business, but that didn't seem to matter as long as we were together. She worked for me for a while, but it wasn't a success. She had no head for figures. Once she left a zero off a big invoice and cost the firm several thousand dollars that it couldn't afford. She tried to learn shorthand but she couldn't seem to grasp that, either.

"She gave up working for me when Nell was on the way, and after that she seemed to resent the business. It was a real thrill for me to work hard and see it grow and know that I'd done it. But she hated it, and she resented me loving it, as well. We ended up fighting about it all the time.''

"And I dare say you spent time being a businessman that you ought to have spent being a husband and father," Gail observed. "You probably couldn't have a night out with her without looking in store windows to see what the competition was doing, and that made her angry."

Steve looked uneasy. "How did you know that?"

"Because when we were in the Lanes you were so absorbed in buying that I could have vanished from the face of the earth and you wouldn't have noticed. Of course—" Gail looked around and dropped her voice, then continued "—we aren't having a real honeymoon, but I expect it would have been all the same if we were." She saw Steve look abashed, and added, "You gave me a present for 'being nice' about it. But if I was in love with you I might not have been so nice about it at all."

Steve was silent a moment before saying wryly, "I think you would have been, because you and I are alike in that respect. You understand obsession. You wouldn't resent the way I never quite forget the business because it's so much like the way you never quite forget your book."

She smiled. "Touché. Tell me some more about Barbara. Had she any brothers or sisters?"

"No, she was an only child."

"What was she interested in?"

He looked vague. "The home, the children—"

"No, I mean when you first met her. What else besides horses?"

"I didn't have much chance to discover her interests, our meetings were so few and brief. But I don't think there *was* much besides horses. Cornelia made sure I saw all the cups and rosettes she'd won. When I was asked to dinner, I thought perhaps Barbara had brought her to our side, but Cornelia's real purpose was to show me what an outsider I was. The entire local old-boy network had been invited, as well, all talking about things that excluded me. We eloped two days later.''

Gail had a vivid inner picture of Barbara, a young woman who'd lived an active life and probably never willingly opened a book, living among strangers, with no inner resources to help her cope. She'd leapt into marriage as though taking a headlong jump, spurred on by her mother's opposition and the excitement of a clandestine romance, but when she'd landed on the other side she'd found herself living with a kind of man she'd never met before. But she'd done her best, trying to join her husband at work and defeated by her own lack of ability.

Her only solace had been her children's love, and she'd tried to claim it all, telling herself her husband cared for nothing but his work. Despite what she'd done to Steve, Gail felt a stab of pity for her. ''Poor Barbara,'' she said.

He looked up, startled. ''What did you say?''

Gail laughed awkwardly. She'd hardly been aware of talking aloud. ''Can't you see that she deserved compassion? She grew up in a safe little world, a local heroine, and then she found herself on the other side of the Atlantic, married to a man who meant well but couldn't see her point of view.'' As Steve stared, Gail added defensively, ''Well, isn't that true? Did you ever wonder if she was having a hard time?''

''I knew there'd be problems at first,'' he said uncertainly, ''but I tried my best.''

''Your best as you saw it, but I wonder how much help it was to her.''

"I loved her," he said quietly. "What more is there?"

Gail considered before saying carefully, "I don't think love on its own is enough. You need understanding, too. Steve, how old were you?"

"Twenty-four," he said wryly, "and I don't need you to tell me that I was about as subtle as a rhinoceros. I doubt I'm much better now."

Gail smiled. "Let's say I don't think putting yourself in other people's shoes is your strong point."

"And it *is* your strong point, I know. But I have a point of view, too."

"But you were on your own home ground. You wouldn't have had half the problems she had. She must have been terribly lonely, and I don't suppose you're an easy man to live with."

"Well, I guess I have to admit that's true." He brooded for a moment, seeming to look into the distance. "I've found it hard to think straight about Barbara. I don't know...." He reddened slightly as he caught her looking at him. "Let's have some more wine."

Gail would have liked to ask more, but he'd closed the subject with an air of finality. "Is that what it means to be a novelist?" he asked as he refilled her glass. "Seeing everyone's point of view."

"Pretty much, yes. I can usually understand how and why a person came to think as he does. It can make life very confusing."

"And what about Harry's point of view? Can you empathise with that?"

She smiled at him over the rim of her glass. "I'm not going to talk about Harry."

"Suppose I'm interested in him?"

"That's just too bad," she responded lightly. "Take my word for it that he isn't in my thoughts."

He grinned. "I wonder a lot about your thoughts, Gail."

"And you'll die wondering," she assured him.

It was late when they wandered back to the hotel along the seashore, listening to the soft splash of the waves. Steve slid an arm about her shoulders, and they drifted along contentedly together. "What shall we do tomorrow?" he asked.

She yawned. "Depends on the weather."

"I'm beginning to understand why the English talk about the weather all the time. You never know from one day to the next what it's going to be."

"I've known snow in July," she confirmed.

"I'll bet you have."

Suddenly Steve stopped and tightened his arm so that she was drawn against him. "Clara Devon is just behind us," he whispered before he laid his lips on hers.

The languorous physical content she'd felt walking beside him was heightened with shocking speed to clamorous desire. The murmur of the sea became a wild thunder in her ears, pounding in time with her heartbeat. The feel of his lips was thrilling. She tried to remember that she was only acting a role, but her whole self was in her answering kiss, and his warm, teasing mouth was giving her an eloquent message.

She felt herself drowning in sensation as he began to rain kisses over her face, murmuring her name in a soft passionate voice. The tremors going through her seemed to take their rhythm from the waves, so that the whole world was beautiful and she was at one with it.

Then his mouth covered hers again, and she parted her lips, inviting him. His tongue made soft teasing movements at first, growing more intense as he felt her supple body mould itself against his, and her sweetness encompass him. He held her close, and closer yet, and now there was no pretence, no questions or answers, only a man and a woman in each other's arms.

Some minutes later, as they prepared to move on, Gail looked for Clara. But the shore was deserted.

CHAPTER SIX

THAT night the heavens opened, but the next day they awoke to find a heat wave. Steve grinned and said, "How about a day on the beach? But pack the umbrella just in case."

The sun scorched down as if determined to make amends for the weather's waywardness. They settled on a huge beach towel, and Gail began to smooth suntan oil over herself. Steve watched her hands moving over her body, delectably revealed by her pink bikini. The two wisps of material were in perfect accord with the character she was projecting, but he was becoming nervously aware that he should have worn a more concealing pair of trunks. "There's an ice cream man over there," he said with relief. "I'll get you one."

He was gone before she had time to say that she never ate ice cream. She finished rubbing in the oil and rolled over onto her stomach, closing her eyes and enjoying the feel of the sun. After a while she felt a strong male hand begin to rub her back. "Hmm," she murmured blissfully, "that's nice."

"I thought you'd like it."

The next moment Gail had rolled over onto her back. *"Harry,"* she exclaimed in dismay. "What on earth are you doing here?"

"I just came to see how you were getting on, darling."

"Don't call me 'darling,'" she said desperately.

Harry was also in bathing trunks that showed off his Adonis looks to perfection. The sun turned his fair hair into a golden halo, and he smiled down at her with the confidence of a man who knew himself to be utterly irresistible. "Just what should I call you?" he said, adding provocatively, "darling."

"You can call me Mrs. Redfern," she said, thoroughly frazzled.

"I shall never think of you as Mrs. Redfern."

Gail lost her patience. "You can *think* of me as Cleopatra if you like, but you will *call* me Mrs. Redfern—when you call me anything. Harry, I'm married now."

"Yes, darling, I know—the first man you bumped into after me. I saw it happen, remember?"

"It's not like that," she said desperately.

"You're not pretending you're in love with him, are you?"

She drew a long breath, knowing she was a long way from being ready for that question. "I don't discuss you with him, and I won't discuss him with you."

"Is he in love with you? He certainly seems to be neglecting you now—"

"He's gone to get me an ice cream," Gail said frantically.

"Damn him!" Harry's voice was savage as befitted a man suffering the hellish pangs of thwarted love. "What right has he to buy you ice cream?"

It was the wrong thing to say. Gail gave a little gasp and pressed her lips together while her eyes, brimming with fun, met Harry's, full of noble suffering. Then she gave up the effort at control and fell back against the towel, laughing until she cried.

"That's wonderful," he snapped. "Go on, jeer at a fellow when he's in torment over you."

Gail mopped her streaming eyes. "I'm sorry, Harry, but you're not in torment. You're just playing a part, only you haven't got a very good script. You shouldn't try to be tragic about ice cream. Oh, heavens!" She began to laugh again.

Harry ground his teeth and looked around uncomfortably at the people on the beach who were beginning to stare at them. "You may feel differently when you know what I came for," he said, lowering his voice and leaning closer to her. "Here." He reached into a small pocket in his trunks and took out some pound notes. "I came to give you what belongs to you."

Gail stared at the money. "What's that?"

"It's repayment of money I owe you. After some of the quite uncalled-for things you said when you walked out on me, I wouldn't dream of keeping a penny that wasn't mine."

Even a casual glance was enough to show Gail that the money was about a quarter of what he owed her. Harry liked his dramatic gestures to be cheap. "You keep it," she said.

"So, suddenly you don't need money? You abandoned me for a rich man?"

"Harry, go away," she said warningly. She'd seen something over his shoulder.

"Not until I've paid you what I owe," he said in a voice that throbbed with drama and, reaching out, he thrust the money into her bikini top. But then, with comic abruptness, he vanished, hauled to his feet by a furious Steve, and the next moment he was wiping ice cream from his face. Gail scrambled up, but before she could speak her hand was seized in a grip of iron and she was being pulled down the beach so fast that her feet barely touched the ground.

Steve halted beside the man hiring pedal boats, paid for an hour's worth and handed Gail in. "Pedal!" he snapped as the man shoved them off.

There was one seat, not quite big enough for the two of them, and they sat pressed up against each other, pedalling furiously until they were far from the shore. Gail felt Steve's thighs rasping against hers, and the heat of his exertion seemed to mingle with her own. The light glittered off the surface of the waves, the sea air was exhilaratingly fresh and salty, and she could sense herself becoming light-headed.

"That's better," Steve said grimly as they slowed. "There isn't another boat in sight so we're actually alone and we can have a talk that's long overdue."

"Steve, don't raise your voice to me, okay?"

"It's far from okay. I'm tired of having to talk in whispers because of who might be listening. For the first time we have some real privacy, so unless there's a Kenleigh spy scuba diving under this boat—which wouldn't surprise me in the slightest—I am free to raise my voice and *I am going to raise my voice.*"

Gail's reply was to get to her feet and dive over the side before he realised what she was going to do. She just heard his yell of alarm before she went under, then the water was singing in her ears and she was floundering. She had a moment's fear at her impulsive action. She was only a moderate swimmer, and if Steve should pedal off in a fury, she was sunk—literally.

But when she got to the surface, he was leaning over the side staring frantically into the water. "What the devil did you do that for?" he yelled.

"Because I don't like being shouted at," she said, getting a firm hold on the boat.

"Take my hand."

"Not until you reform."

He ground his teeth. "For the love of heaven, Gail, will you take my hand?"

"Do you promise?"

"It would serve you right if I went off and left you, you harpy."

"Goodbye," she said cheerfully. She knew now that he wouldn't abandon her.

He met her laughing eyes, and there was the hint of an answering gleam in his own. "Think you can swim back to shore?" he asked.

She considered. "I got my hundred-yard certificate at school."

He burst into a bellow of laughter and reached out his hand to her. "Get in," he said.

She let him hoist her aboard and steady her as she squeezed back into the confined space beside him. The feel of his hands on her waist gave her the sensation of being totally naked instead of only nearly so.

"You're the craziest woman I've ever known," Steve exclaimed, trying to sound annoyed to cover the fact that he'd had a fright, and not quite succeeding.

"I was just checking under the boat," she said impishly. "You'll be glad to know there's no Kenleigh spy there." She wrung out her hair and looked down to find that Harry's money was miraculously still tucked into her bikini top. Steve followed her glance and was there before her, sliding his fingers beneath the material and withdrawing the sodden notes. Before Gail realised what he was going to do, he'd tossed them into the water.

"Hey!" she yelled indignantly, leaping to her feet, but Steve's hands closed on her waist, the fingers almost meeting around it, and he pulled her back down beside him.

"I don't like you taking money from him," he said.

"Will you let go of me, please?"

"No."

"It wasn't his money, it was mine—money that he owed me."

"I'll refund it to you."

"That's not the point. What you just did was high-handed and dictatorial—"

"Then it's just as well I've got a good firm hold on you, isn't it?"

He was indeed holding on to her very firmly, with hands that seemed to scorch her skin, setting off trails of heat that ran through her, making it suddenly hard to breathe. She wished the rise and fall of her breasts wasn't so evident. She tried to push against his chest but it remained unyielding. His face was close, and there was a glint in his eye that was part anger, part something else. "He could have sent you that money by check," Steve said. "There was no need to follow you on your honeymoon. You invited him here, didn't you?"

"Are you out of your mind?"

"The night we arrived I stayed awake all night. That's how I know you crept into the bathroom when you thought I was asleep. You left the door ajar, so when you'd been in there an hour I went to investigate and found you scribbling away at something. Four days later Harry turns up. A coincidence? Not on your life! And to think I was fool enough to believe you when you said he wasn't in your thoughts!"

Gail was too incensed to pay much attention to the sudden note of bitterness in his voice. "Leave my thoughts out of this," she snapped. "They don't come into our agreement. Do you really think I was writing to Harry and asking him to follow us? A fine opinion you have of me!"

"I don't know what to think about you, Gail. We're complete and utter strangers."

"I wasn't writing to Harry. I happen to believe in keeping my word."

"To the letter, yes, but what about the spirit? You're in love with him, which means you'll interpret the rules in your own way."

Gail glared. Steve waited for her to speak, but before she could do so her face changed and assumed an abstracted expression, as though she was listening to faraway music. "Gail, are you with me?" he demanded.

"Yes, sorry," she said hastily. "It's just that I suddenly realised how misunderstandings happen. I never use them in my plots because I get exasperated, thinking, 'Why didn't they just explain everything to each other?' But you've shown me the answer."

"Well, that's just dandy," he said, wondering if he was going mad. "Are you going to tell me what you're talking about, or is this a guessing game?"

"You just made me so cross with your damn fool accusations that I'm tempted not to explain what I was writing. It would serve you right if I just let you stew."

"Oh, really?"

"Yes, but I won't yield to that temptation because misunderstandings are a bore in real life. In fact, they're a bore in books, too, but—"

"Gail," he said dangerously, making a movement that caused the pedal boat to rock.

PLAY THE
LUCKY CARNIVAL WHEEL
and get as many as
SIX FREE GIFTS..

HOW TO PLAY:

1. With a coin, carefully scratch away the silver panel opposite. Then check your number against the numbers opposite to find out how many gifts you're eligible to receive.

2. You'll receive brand-new Mills & Boon Romances and possibly other gifts - ABSOLUTELY FREE! Return this card today and we'll promptly send you the free books and the gifts you've qualified for!

3. We're sure that, after your specially selected free books. you'll want more of these heartwarming Romances. So unless we hear otherwise, every month we will send you our 6 latest Romances for just £1.80 each * - the same price in the shops. Postage and Packing are free - we pay all the extras!
* Please note prices may be subject to VAT.

4. Your satisfaction is guaranteed! You may cancel or suspend your subscription at any time, simply by writing to us. The free books and gifts remain yours to keep.

NO COST! NO RISKS!
NO OBLIGATION TO BUY

FREE! THIS CUDDLY TEDDY BEAR!

You'll love this little teddy bear. He's soft and cuddly with an adorable expression that's sure to make you smile.

Mills & Boon Reader Service
FREEPOST
P.O. Box 236
Croydon
Surrey
CR9 9EL

NO
STAMP
NEEDED

"All right, I'm coming to the point. I wasn't writing to Harry. Will you please get it into your head that I'm not in love with him anymore? In fact, I never was. It's all over."

"Rather sudden, isn't it?" Steve asked. Inwardly he was holding his breath.

"No, it only looks that way. I really got over him ages ago, but it took the other night to make me realise it. He was never really in love with me, either."

"Then why does he keep coming around?"

"Because no one's ever taken anything away from him before and he can't understand it. Steve, will you please forget about Harry?"

"How can I forget him when he keeps turning up?" Steve demanded reasonably.

"What you saw me writing were notes for my book. I awoke with a brilliant idea that I had to get down while it was fresh."

He stared. "Are you telling me that with everything that was happening, your mind was still working on your book?"

"But I told you before, part of my mind is *always* working, watching every situation to see if there's something I can use. Take the night we met, when I thought you were attacking me. I fought you but I didn't scream. In thrillers the heroine always does both, but I discovered you can't. You haven't got enough breath." She chuckled at his incredulous expression. "It was really a very useful experience."

"You were making notes while we were struggling?" Steve demanded, dazed.

"Subconsciously, yes, although I didn't realise it until later."

"Well, I'm glad to know I've been useful," he said with heavy irony.

"I knew you would be," Gail said with a demureness that made him look at her suspiciously. She disconcerted him like a firecracker that might go off in any direction without warning.

"And when you kissed me in front of the waiter, that was just another form of note taking?" he asked casually.

She thought of the excitement that had streamed through her body at the touch of his lips, the ache in her breasts at the feel of him pressed close to her, and her throat tightened so that she had to calm herself before she could speak. At last she managed to say, "Of course."

Steve moved one hand to her shoulders, leaving the other on her waist. Then he tightened them, pulling her hard against him. With his free hand he drew her chin around so that her face was close to his, and she had a close-up view of his eyes blazing with something that was far more unnerving than anger. "Steve—"

"Just think of it as an enlargement of your experience," he said. "You can make the notes later." On the last word he locked his mouth onto hers. Overhead, the vivid blue sky swam. The boat seemed to rock beneath her—or perhaps it was the world that had rocked as he held her naked flesh hard against his. Gail clung to him with hands that found their place naturally on his body, and sweetness flooded her as she felt herself moulded against him.

She'd told herself that they were acting in character, but this was no role-playing, and now she knew they'd both been waiting for the chance to discover each other more completely. It had been inevitable from the moment he'd first laid his lips on hers, perhaps from the moment she'd first seen him and been secretly tempted.

He pressed her against the cushions, and the back of the seat yielded until they were almost reclining. Steve was trailing his tongue along the line of her jaw until he found the angle and teased the soft skin below her ear, making her gasp. Pleasure streamed throughout her body, and she instinctively arched against him, seeking deeper satisfaction.

At once she felt Steve working at the fastening of her bikini top, releasing it, drawing the minute garment forward, then a sensation of agonised delight as he brushed his fingers against the nipple. She found the wits to murmur, "Steve, we're out in plain view—"

"We're a mile from the shore, and we have the world to ourselves," he said against her mouth. A note of devilment came into his voice as he added, "Are you storing all this for future reference?"

"Oh, shut up," she murmured, and felt his answering chuckle.

He teased the nipple into a peak of expectancy. Gail trembled at that sweet-sharp feeling and abandoned her last hold on reason. Pulling his head down, she kissed him hungrily, letting her lips and hands tell him of her passion. She felt the jerk of shock in Steve's body as their mutual desire flared into one flame, devouring them both together. He drew back to look down on her as she lay there, golden and glowing, and shook his head a little. Then a little smile touched his lips. "Does Drake Domino do it like that?" he asked.

"He doesn't believe in female entanglements," Gail said slowly. "He thinks they addle a man's wits."

"He's right," Steve said. He drew a ragged breath. "Gail, come back with me—to the hotel."

"Yes," she murmured. "Oh, yes."

They turned the boat and headed back to the shore. Gail's blood was singing, less from the exercise than the eager thought of what was to come. They beached the boat and ran to collect their things. They were in too much of a hurry to dress fully. Steve drew on a shirt, and Gail flung a light beach coat over her bikini for the short trip back to the hotel.

There were two other people in the lift to their floor, so they were forced to stand sedately, watching each other, smiling. As soon as the door of the bridal suite had closed behind them, Steve seized her in a crushing embrace.

And she yelled.

Steve jumped back, rubbing his left ear, which had taken the full force of her shout. "What's the matter?" he said, bewildered. "How could I have hurt you?"

Gail opened her beach coat. Aghast, they both gazed down at her exposed skin, which was already turning a bright lobster red. "Oh, no!" she said in despair. "I should have known—my skin's so fair."

"You mean that always happens?"

"No, it must have been because we went out in the boat," she said, almost weeping with frustration. "The glare of the sea makes the sun's rays more intense. Oh, heavens, I'm on fire." She looked down at her scarlet skin, and the ironic humour that was never far from the surface made her add bitterly, "I *would* choose today to wear shocking pink, wouldn't I?"

Steve grinned in appreciation of her resilience. "Have you got anything soothing to rub in?" he asked sympathetically.

"Not with me." She touched her shoulder delicately and winced.

"All right, leave it to me. Get in the shower until I come back."

He vanished out of the door. Moving with great care, Gail took off the tiny bikini and got under a cool shower. She was burned extensively in the front, her shoulders and arms and halfway down her back. From there downward she'd been protected by the fact that she was sitting down. She groaned, less with pain than with exasperation at her misfortunes.

It was impossible to wrap the towel around her, so she stood there dabbing herself carefully, an inch at a time, so absorbed that she didn't hear Steve's return. She looked up in despair as he entered the bathroom. She'd wanted him to see her naked, but not painted lobster red.

"I'll do that," he said. "Carefully now." He dabbed her down gently, impersonally, seeming not to notice that she was naked. Gail wondered miserably if he was being kind or if her unusual body decoration had put him right off the idea. "I've got something that the store clerk swore would soothe the pain away," he said. "Come and lie down, and I'll put it on you."

"Steve, I can—"

"Lie down," he said firmly.

She gave up the struggle and lay on her back while he poured the soothing oil over her. It was blissful. Gradually the pain faded and there was only the feeling of Steve's hands moving smoothly and purposefully over her. She met his eyes and found only warmth there. "Oh, hell!" she said.

He laughed. "It can't be helped. Turn over."

She rolled onto her stomach, and Steve smoothed the oil down her back to where the burning faded. Then there was silence, and after a moment she felt Steve's hand drift lower, encompassing one perfectly rounded buttock. "You do have a fair skin, don't you?" he observed. "A beautiful English rose."

"I can't be beautiful if I'm lobster red," she murmured sleepily.

Steve patted her behind. "You're beautiful there," he teased.

Gail was suffused with warmth and growing sleepy. She dropped her head onto the pillow and let herself sink contentedly down into the darkness. The last thing she was aware of was a faint touch on each buttock, as though someone had kissed them.

She awoke three hours later, feeling much better, although still unusually warm. Steve was sitting in the window reading a newspaper. He looked up smiling, and she realised she was still naked. She swung her legs out of bed and slipped on the light beach coat. "Isn't it a little late for that?" he asked quizzically.

She laughed, wondering why she could feel a blush rising in her face, but before she could answer him, the telephone rang. Steve answered it, and Gail saw his face go very pale. At last he exploded, *"Damn them!"* He looked at Gail. "You suspected they were planning something, didn't you? They're trying to take Nell and Kevin abroad."

"What?" She took the phone from him. "Leonard, what's happened?"

"The Kenleighs have applied to the court for permission to take the children to France for a holiday," the old man told her. "And they've sneakily got a last-minute hearing set for tomorrow. I've entered an objection, but you'd better get back here quick. Once those children are abroad, they're out of the court's jurisdiction, and there's no guarantee they'll ever come back."

Gail looked at Steve. The wonderful hours of this morning were wiped out. His face was haggard again, his eyes desperate, and she was consumed with a sudden cold fury such as she'd never known before in her life. How *dared* they do this to him!

"Leonard," she said crisply, "will you please enter an immediate counter application? Mr. Redfern wishes his children to spend the summer holiday in the cottage with him. He now has a wife who is capable of making a proper home for them all, and if Mr. Brace has any ideas about trying to prove our marriage a sham, refer him to Miss Clara Devon, who can tell him a few things that will make his heart sink.

"You can also make it plain that we're prepared to call Miss Devon as a witness, and I can give you her number if you wish to telephone her today."

Leonard's crack of triumphant laughter came down the line, but she hardly heard it. Her eyes were on Steve, looking at her as if he'd just seen her for the first time.

CHAPTER SEVEN

THEY returned to Chalmley that evening. The next day they arrived at court to find Leonard waiting for them. "Well done," he said to Gail. "I gather you caught Brace's agent and turned her."

"I don't know that I actually turned her around to our side," Gail said, "but I think I made her useless to them."

Leonard nodded. "Brace didn't like my knowing so much about her. There won't be any trouble about the marriage today."

The Kenleighs were there with Mr. Brace, who avoided Gail's eye. There was, mercifully, no sign of the children.

There was a rustle in the courtroom as the judge made his entrance. He was a middle-aged man with a hard face that made an instantly disagreeable impression on Gail. He gave a thin smile in the direction of the Kenleighs, whom he obviously recognised. Steve saw it and muttered bitterly, "Old boy." For once Gail feared he might be right.

As they all sat down, the judge leaned towards his clerk and said something that Gail couldn't hear. But reading his lips she thought she understood, "Hope this won't take too long." Her heart sank. How could they hope for sympathetic understanding from this man?

The hearing began. Mr. Brace delivered a short, eloquent speech, making the Kenleighs' position seem so entirely reasonable that Gail became apprehensive. Steve was tense and silent beside her.

Leonard rose and said that his client sought the opportunity to re-establish his relationship with his children, which he was being improperly denied. He spoke bluntly, with none of Mr. Brace's suave assurance, and the judge hardly seemed to be listening.

Lady Kenleigh whispered to Mr. Brace, who rose and said there was a practical objection, as the cottage was too small to sleep two extra. Gail immediately nudged Leonard and muttered, "Call me."

"I believe Mrs. Redfern can answer the objection, Your Honour," Leonard said.

"There's an unused room in the cottage that can easily be equipped as a bedroom," Gail explained. "I intend to see to it immediately."

The judge said "Hmm!" but made no other comment, and Gail sat down, feeling she hadn't done any real good. She slipped her hand into Steve's. They both waited tensely for the judge to question them further, and she sent up a little prayer that Steve would keep his temper.

But without further ado the judge announced, "I have to say that Mr. Redfern's contact with his children seems to have been very limited until now. It's hard to see how a satisfactory parent-child bond can have been maintained. Therefore—"

The Kenleighs were already smiling, sure of victory. Steve's hand tightened on Gail's, and she turned to him, her heart aching for his suffering.

"Therefore," the judge continued, "I consider it advisable for the children to spend the weeks of the school holiday with Mr. and Mrs. Redfern with a view to seeing whether such a bond can be reestablished before custody is finally decided."

It took a moment for the truth to sink in. Then, with one impulse, Steve and Gail flung themselves into each other's arms, clinging together in speechless joy. They didn't hear the judge adding a rider about not removing Nell and Kevin from the court's jurisdiction. They'd forgotten everything but their shared happiness—the happiness of comrades who'd fought a good battle side-by-side. Steve's eyes were shining with gratitude.

Over his shoulder Gail caught a glimpse of the Kenleighs leaving the court. Lady Kenleigh was weeping, and Gail had a sudden disconcerting moment of anger at Sir William, who was lingering several steps behind his wife, trying to seem unaware of her tears. *Help her, damn you,* Gail thought. Then they passed out of sight.

The three of them celebrated over a champagne lunch, but Gail found her pleasure was slightly dimmed by the memory of Lady Kenleigh's face and her husband's cool indifference. She still had no doubts about Steve's right to his children, but Lady Kenleigh was no longer the villain of the piece.

"This is going to be a tough arrangement for you," Steve commented when they were at home that evening. "That room was going to be yours to work in."

"I'll manage," she assured him. "I can work in the bedroom."

She went to the furniture shop the next day. Steve, overjoyed at the prospect of having Nell and Kevin living with him again, came with her and drove her mad by worrying about each small decision. "Steve," she said once, frazzled, "we're buying a couple of beds for a couple of kids, not purchasing the crown jewels. As long as the mattresses are comfortable they won't care if the headboard is walnut or pine.''

"I just want everything to be perfect," he said. "It's been so long...."

"I know. But what'll make it perfect for them is being with you. Just let them know that you love them, and you *can't* go wrong."

He enjoyed himself in the toy department, choosing gifts to welcome his children, and Gail watched him, smiling tenderly at his happiness, yet feeling sad for him when he had to ask, "What would a ten-year-old-girl like?"

"Well," said the saleswoman, "if it's a child you don't know well—"

"It used to be so easy buying for girls," Gail put in quickly, seeing the shadow on Steve's face, "but lots of them don't like dolls now. They prefer cowboy outfits."

"Well, I'm sure as hell not buying a doll for Kevin," Steve said, startled.

In the end he bought far too much, trying to cover all possibilities, but Gail didn't attempt to restrain him. She knew he needed some outlet for his feelings.

Her own feelings had strands of dismay and disappointment mingled with them. At Brighton there'd been just the two of them, discovering each other and beginning to explore passion. But now the thought of his children seemed to have driven everything else from Steve's mind. It seemed as if a feeling that was so potentially explosive for her had been no more than a distraction to Steve.

When they left, instead of heading for home, Steve took her to the best computer shop in Chalmley. "It's about time you had that word processor."

He guided her to the model he'd installed in his stores and showed her what it could do for her with a completeness that had the salesman wringing his hands in frustration. Gail lost her heart to the powerful machine that could make her work so much easier, but the price was far too high.

But Steve simply told the salesman to deliver it and offered his own credit card. "No, Steve," Gail pleaded. "I can't take any more from you."

"Any more?" he echoed. "Don't you know that I've given you nothing beside what you've given me? Let me give you something Gail, something that isn't just money."

"All right," she said happily. She spent the journey home in a blissful reverie about floppy disks and formats.

There was a week to go until the start of the school holidays. Steve hired a woman to do the daily cooking and cleaning so that Gail would be free to write, but they had to do the extra themselves. Between them they managed to clean the spare room and paint the walls, and when the new carpet had been laid, the beds made up and the presents laid out, the room looked as bright and welcoming as any child could wish.

On the last evening, they sat in jeans and sweatshirts in the kitchen, worn out, drinking beer and munching sandwiches. "We did it," Steve said with his eyes closed.

"Mmm." Gail salvaged a crumb.

"What's the time? I'm too tired to look."

"Steve," she said gently, "it's five minutes later than it was the last time you asked. Tomorrow won't get here any faster that way."

"But they *will* come, won't they? You don't think the Kenleighs will find a new way to stop them?"

She gave a faint chuckle. "Not after that letter Leonard wrote."

Steve grinned. "Yes, the old boy practically threatened them with the Tower of London. Are you coming with me when I collect them?"

"I don't think so. You need to be alone with them."

"Yes." He sounded uneasy.

"You've got to get to know them again. I'll just fade into the background."

"Of course," he said hastily. "I promised you I'd ask nothing from you but the formality, and I've already broken that promise a dozen times over. You've been very generous, especially after what happened."

"What do you mean?"

"The way I acted on the pedal boat—in fact right through our honeymoon—was inexcusable. Your working methods are your own affair, and I had no business to get annoyed about them or—or anything else you do."

"Steve—" Gail began.

"No, let me get this out. I've been trying to find the courage for days, so don't stop me. Since we came back and you've been so marvellous—the court appearance and everything—I've come to see that I acted like a Grade A, twenty-four-carat jerk."

"That's perfectly all right," she said in a colourless voice.

"It's not all right until you say you forgive me. Well, I guess I know you have, but I'd like to hear the words."

"In that case, I forgive you."

He stretched out his hand. "Friends?"

After a moment she took it. "Friends."

"I had to say it tonight because when Nell and Kevin are here I can't go on sleeping on the sofa and I'll have to move in with you. But I want you to know that—"

"Steve, it's really all right. I've got the point."

"Fine." He grinned suddenly. "No misunderstandings."

"None at all," she said cheerfully.

Steve drove off the next morning and was away so long that Gail was afraid something had gone wrong. But at last the car drew up outside the cottage and Nell got out, followed by Kevin, clutching a madly wriggling puppy. Gail went outside and stood on the step. Now the moment had come, she realised, that these children were likely to eye their father's new wife askance. But while their greeting was reserved, there was no hostility in their manner, and Kevin held out the puppy, declaring, "This is Samantha, but we call her Sammi."

Gail took the frantic little bundle into her arms and was rewarded by having a nose like an ice cube pressed against her cheek. Nell and Kevin smiled, evidently taking this as a mark of canine esteem, and the awkwardness of the moment was lost in puppy talk. As they all moved into the house, Steve muttered to Gail, "Cornelia gave them the pup yesterday. You can guess why."

"Never mind," she said soothingly. "The more the merrier."

Milk and sandwiches got them over the next hurdle, then there was the bedroom to be looked at and presents to be exclaimed over. Sammi christened the new carpet, and in the consternation and laughter the mood eased a little more. Gail began to hope that everything would go smoothly.

But she'd relaxed too soon. A little later she and Steve looked into the children's room to see if they were settling in. They arrived just in time to see Nell slide something hastily under her pillow. But in her urgency she pushed it too hard, and it slid out the other side onto the floor. It was the photograph of Barbara that Gail had seen at the centre of the shrine at Kenleigh Grange. As the children saw their father's eyes alight on it, they stared at him with a touch of defiance.

"I don't think that's very kind," Steve said, "when Gail's gone to so much trouble to make things nice for you."

"But it's lovely," Gail put in quickly, before he could make matters worse. She picked up the picture to study it. "It's your mother, isn't it?"

They nodded, silent. They both had the wariness of children who'd learned that least said was the best way to survive adult pressure. Gail hurt inwardly for them. "She's only been dead a few months," she said gently. "Of course, you want to keep her with you." She smiled at Kevin. "You're very like her."

The child's face relaxed, but before he could speak, Nell put in, "I'm like her, too. Grandma says so."

"I can't see it," Steve said, puzzled.

"Well, I can," Gail said, throwing him a dark look. "Nell has her mother's beautiful eyes."

In fact there wasn't the slightest resemblance, but Gail's empathy had taken her into the little girl's heart and shown her Nell's aching sense of loss and her longing to emulate her mother's attractiveness. Gail had confirmation in the look on Nell's face, part pleasure and part sheer surprise at being understood.

Gail placed the picture on the small table between the two beds. "Why don't you keep her there, where you can see her all the time?'' she suggested, smiling. She took Steve's hand and drew him from the room before he could do any more damage.

"Don't make them take sides, Steve," she said urgently when they were alone. "They shouldn't have to hide their mother's picture from their father as if it was a guilty secret."

He sighed. "I guess I just hoped things were going to be different now."

"But what do you mean by 'different'? You can't write Barbara out of their past. They're her children, too."

He flushed with sudden anger. "They also happen to be mine, and I think I know how to handle them," he said sharply. "I'm grateful for what you just did, but please don't try to tell me how to run my family."

Gail dropped her hand away from him. "I'll see how the tea is coming on," she said quietly, and turned to go down to the kitchen. Steve stayed where he was on the stairs, cursing himself for his clumsiness, wishing he could find words for his dismay and confusion and knowing he'd alienated the one person who could have explained them to him.

He was furious with Gail. Barbara's picture had made him indignant on her behalf, but when he'd tried to defend her she'd snubbed him, reminding him that she wasn't his real wife and didn't need his defence. The pain of that snub had made him lash out, but when he'd seen the life drain out of her face, her unhappiness had somehow come back to him, hurting him more than his own. Gradually his anger turned from her to himself.

He followed her into the kitchen a few minutes later. "You shouldn't have to do this," he said awkwardly, indicating the cooking. "It wasn't part of our agreement."

She almost said bitterly, "To hell with the agreement," but controlled her tongue and said, "It's only for this one day. Mrs. Jones will be in tomorrow." It had been her own suggestion that the housekeeper take today off so that as few people as possible would be there for the difficult first day.

Against his will he had a sharp memory of the glamorously dressed creature in the bridal suite. Today she was in functional jeans and an overlarge shirt buttoned up to the neck. Her sunburn had faded to an attractive light tan, but she looked tired, and somehow she affected him more. The other woman had been a fiction; this was Gail, a real person who'd lavished her generosity on him and whom he'd hurt.

He could have put out a hand and touched her, but he had a sharp sensation of the distance between them. "Look," he said awkwardly, "I just want you to know that I appreciate this and...everything...it's just—"

"It's all right, I'm not going to interfere," she assured him.

"That's not what I—"

"Hush," Gail said urgently. She'd seen the door opening. A moment later the children, silent as ghosts, slid inside and stood there expectantly, gauging the atmosphere. Gail saw Kevin's hand slide into his sister's.

The conversation over tea was a mine field. Nell and Kevin avoided mentioning Kenleigh Grange or their grandparents, and as they knew the locality better than Steve himself, there wasn't much inspiration to be found there, either. Samantha saved the day by going around begging from everyone in turn, and their laughter covered the silence that otherwise would have yawned. "We must buy her a bed," Gail said, "and some toys."

"Fine, a shopping trip after we finish," Steve said cheerfully.

"You'd better get some dog food, as well," Gail reflected. "I'll give you a list."

"But aren't you coming?" Kevin asked.

"I have to do the washing up," she improvised hastily.

"If I helped you with it, you could come with us," Nell insisted.

"But I'm not dressed to go out," Gail said desperately.

"So get changed," Steve told her.

"If I've got to change and wash up, the shops will soon be closed," Gail remarked. "Of course, *you* could wash up."

"I could, couldn't I?" he agreed without enthusiasm. He caught his daughter looking at him and added defensively, "I *do* know how to wash up."

"Does he?" Gail asked, seeing Nell's dubious face.

Nell shook her head, her eyes gleaming with childish mischief for the first time. Steve appealed to his son for support. "Can *you* wash up?"

Kevin shook his head vigorously and promptly steered the conversation away from danger by telling Gail solemnly, "I think you're pretty like you are."

"Good work," Steve commended him. "Always distract a woman with a compliment."

Father and son shook hands solemnly. Nell laughed, and Gail felt a sudden sense of happiness. This visit would have its troubles, but it could work, because underlying it was the bond that still united Steve with his children. It had briefly surfaced for a light-hearted moment, and surely there'd be other, deeper ones.

Steve got to work in the kitchen with more willingness and skill than he'd led her to believe, and Gail went upstairs to dress. When she came out of her room she found Nell waiting for her. "I wanted to ask you," the little girl said hurriedly, "what shall we call you?"

"Why don't you call me Gail?"

"You won't . . . mind that?" Nell asked cautiously.

For a moment Gail was puzzled. Then she realised Nell had dreaded being asked to call her Mummy. "I think Gail is nice and friendly," she said, smiling as warmly as she could to show that everything was all right.

Nell beamed and skipped down the stairs to where Kevin was waiting and muttered something in his ear. He nodded, also beaming.

Gail managed to get Steve alone for a moment to tell him what had been decided, and to add, "I shan't come out with the three of you after this. You'll have them all to yourself."

They had a successful shopping trip and returned laden with a bean bed, a blanket, three different kinds of food and virtually the entire contents of the pet shop's toy department. These were offered to Samantha one by one, but she rejected them all in favour of the brush that she'd purloined for herself from the cupboard under the sink.

Gail had made a few small purchases of her own, and on the pretext of helping her with them, Nell came up to her room. She was fascinated by the corner table Gail had turned into a mini-study and by the computer that still stood in its box on the floor. "That's the same kind

Daddy has,'' she exclaimed, reading the details off the side.

''Yes, he gave it to me,'' Gail said unguardedly.

''You mean—as a wedding present?'' Nell asked, frowning.

''Well…yes…sort of,'' Gail admitted, wishing she'd thought before she spoke.

''Daddy gave you a *computer* as a wedding present?'' Nell echoed, scandalised.

''Why not?'' Gail said, trying to sound airy. ''A present ought to be what you most want, and that was what I most wanted. I write books, and getting words down is a terrible chore without a machine.''

At once Nell was eager. ''You write books—I mean, publishers accept them and actually publish them?''

''One publisher, and so far only two books,'' Gail said, laughing. ''But I'm doing a third.''

''But you're a *real* author. Can I see your books?''

Gail rummaged through a box and found a copy of the first one. Nell reached out eager hands, but at the last minute she rubbed them on her jeans before taking the book reverently. She placed it on the bed and began to turn the pages, and Gail watched her in amazement. Surely children didn't regard books with that kind of awe these days? Pop records, yes; clothes, yes. But books? ''Do you read very much?'' she asked.

''Lots and lots,'' Nell said. ''Grandma says I read too much, but I love reading. It's so exciting when you get right into a story, and it makes you forget the outside world.''

''Yes, that's how I felt when I was your age,'' Gail agreed, remembering how much she'd needed an escape and how eagerly she'd plunged into books to find it.

"It's got your picture on the back," Nell exclaimed in thrilled discovery.

"Would you like to have the book?"

The child's eyes shone. "Can I really have it? Would you sign it?"

Gail laughed. "Of course, if you like."

"And will you put my name, so that everyone knows it's meant for me and nobody else?"

Touched, Gail took her pen and wrote, "To my friend Nell, with love from Gail." Nell was almost speechless with joy and gratitude. Gail looked at her examining the dust jacket and felt that Nell would be an interesting person to know.

"It's about murder!" Nell exclaimed in delight as she studied the artistic, red-dripping stiletto on the front cover.

"Well, it's a mystery story," Gail said cautiously.

"But there *is* a body," Nell insisted, as if fearful of being done out of a treat. "It says so on the jacket."

"There are two bodies," Gail reassured her.

"Do they get horribly murdered?" Nell demanded with relish.

"Horribly," Gail promised, realising that it would be useless to say anything else.

Nell's cup of bliss appeared to run over. She insisted on taking the book to supper and showed it to Kevin, explaining that Gail was a *real* writer. The little boy was loftily unimpressed. "I expect it's just a soppy love story," he said.

"It isn't," Nell declared, outraged by this slander. "It's all about murder, and there are simply masses of bodies and oodles of blood."

Gail turned away, her lips twitching, and caught Steve's eye. He looked at her quizzically. ''Don't blame me,'' she murmured.

Over supper Nell clamored to be told about Drake Domino, and Gail obliged. ''He's an Edwardian,'' she explained.

''What's that?'' Kevin demanded.

''Someone who lived when Edward VII was on the throne,'' Nell informed him. ''I've just been learning about him. He was the son of Queen Victoria, and he was king eighty years ago. He got very fat, he liked enjoying himself, and he was in love with lots of ladies.''

''History lessons have certainly improved since I was at school,'' Gail remarked, amused. ''We just did boring dates. The teacher didn't mention 'lots of ladies.' ''

''Well, actually, our teacher didn't mention them, either,'' confessed Nell.

''I expect you found that in a book,'' Gail suggested.

Nell nodded. ''It was a book I wasn't supposed to be reading,'' she added, as though that added the last drop of pleasure. It was a pleasure Gail had once known well. She laughed, and for a moment her eyes met Nell's in pure understanding.

''I don't ever remember reading a book out of school,'' Steve said. ''Certainly not history. I hated it.''

''But it's wonderful,'' Nell protested. ''It's full of exciting things like kings and queens and all the wicked things they did—''

''History's all scandal to you, isn't it?'' Gail broke in quickly. She'd seen Steve's face darken.

''Scandals are the most fun,'' Nell said unanswerably.

"Anyway, Drake Domino is an Edwardian aristo-crat," Gail said, hurrying on, "and he solves his crimes by observation and deduction, like Sherlock Holmes."

"Who's Sherlock Holmes?" Kevin asked.

"I'll tell you later," Nell whispered repressively. "Now hush!"

Kevin obediently subsided.

"Does he have an arch opponent?" Nell asked melodramatically.

"Yes, Drake Domino's fiendish enemy is called Professor Savernake."

After that Gail kept the conversation in safer chan-nels, and there was only one other awkward moment. Just before Nell went to bed she clutched the book to her and said eagerly, "Just wait until I show this to the other girls at school." Steve managed a smile, but he was very silent.

Later, when Gail had seen the children tucked in, she came downstairs to find Steve drinking a large whis-key. "They've turned her into a real English child, haven't they?" he said bitterly. "Before you know where you are, they'll both be part of the old-boy net-work. Kings and queens indeed!"

"Don't read anything into that," she urged. "Chil-dren enjoy colourful things. Presidents may have vir-tue on their side, but royalty is more fun."

Steve gave a short laugh and said wryly, "I guess so. It's not really that . . ." He trailed off.

"I know," Gail said sympathetically, "it was her ca-sual remark about going back to school."

"I'm fighting to take them away from here. If I have my way, she'll never see that school again, but she talked as though she wanted to go back to it."

"Steve, she spoke without thinking. You mustn't torment yourself over every word like this, it isn't fair to them. Try to be natural with them—and forget about your race prejudice."

"My *what*?"

"You're so anti-English. You haven't got a good word for any of us, and you know nothing about us. Your ideas come out of a time warp. Admittedly the Kenleighs are a bit old-fashioned. Most of us don't have grand libraries or riding lessons. But I'll bet you contributed your own bit of prejudice."

"And just what's that supposed to mean?" Steve demanded. Gail noted with pleasure that indignation had taken his mind off his gloom.

"It means that when you first arrived here you were probably surprised to see policemen in modern uniforms," she said, pressing home the attack with relish. "I'll bet you thought we were policed by the Beefeaters in the Tower of London."

Steve opened his mouth to protest, then closed it again.

"Nell and Kevin are half English, and they're just as much entitled to learn about their mother's heritage as their father's. And another thing, I've lived here since I was born, and the only person I've ever heard use the expression 'old-boy network' is *you*—old boy!"

In the silence that followed Steve stared at her, then a slow grin spread over his face. "Well, that's telling me," he remarked. "Race-prejudiced, eh? And I never knew it."

"You see us all in stereotypes and you don't give us a chance."

"Well, perhaps that's true," he said reflectively. "But then, perhaps you ought to consider how much you've done to confirm my prejudices?"

"Me?" Gail exclaimed, but then she saw that Steve was smiling in a disturbing way.

"Of course, you," he said. "Isn't there a stereotype of the beautiful English rose? And didn't you confirm it for me the first moment I saw you?"

While she was still trying to think of an answer, he leaned over and brushed his lips lightly against hers. "Now, Mrs. Redfern, perhaps we should turn in. I don't know about you, but the day has left me exhausted."

They looked into the children's room. " 'Night, kids," Steve said.

"Good night, Daddy," came two dutiful voices.

"Do you want anything before I turn in?" Gail asked.

"No, thank you."

Steve closed the door and looked at Gail. "You see?" he sighed. "At one time they'd have been all over me when I looked in last thing— Now what's so funny?"

"Don't you realise we were being got rid of?" Gail chuckled. "Or why?"

"No, tell me why."

But she didn't have to. A muffled yap from behind the door gave the game away. Steve looked in again and switched on the light. "Okay, where is she?"

"Where's who?" Kevin asked innocently.

But Sammi spoiled it by sticking the end of her nose above the sheet. Steve pulled the sheet back and discovered her regarding him with two beady eyes.

"Please, Daddy," came a protesting chorus.

"Dogs sleep downstairs in the kitchen," he said firmly.

"But she was crying," Kevin protested.

"That's because it's her first night away from her mother. She'll get used to it, as all pups do. Come on."

Reluctantly Kevin handed Sammi over, and Steve tucked her under his arm. "Go to sleep," he said, and closed the door behind him.

"Now I suppose they really *do* think I'm a monster," he growled as they returned to the kitchen. "But I couldn't let Kevin sleep with a dog. It isn't healthy."

"Are you sure that's the only reason?" Gail asked.

Steve looked up from settling the pup on her bean bed. "What's that supposed to mean?"

"Sammi was a gift from the Kenleighs, wasn't she?"

"And they're a sight more interested in her than anything I bought them," he said bitterly. "But that has nothing to do with it."

"If you say so."

"Gail, *it has nothing to do with it*."

"All right, all right."

She'd wondered how they would manage in the bed upstairs. Although a double bed, it was much narrower than the huge one in the bridal suite, and it was impossible not to be aware of Steve only a few inches away, the warmth of his body reaching her. She lay awake for a long time, listening to Sammi wailing below. "Your children aren't the only ones who think you're a monster," she whispered. "Listen to that poor little thing. I'm going down to her."

His hand on her arm restrained her. "I'd rather you didn't. Gail, you have to be firm with dogs."

"But it's her first night."

"That's what Barbara always said, and that's how we ended up with dogs ruling the house. You've got to start as you mean to go on."

She sighed and tried to tell herself that it wasn't really her business. After a while she fell into a light sleep through which she could still hear the pup sobbing bitterly. Then the sobs stopped with an abruptness that made her wake up.

She was alone. She got out of bed and went out onto the landing, where the dim light showed her Nell and Kevin standing on the stairs, leaning over and staring at something that evidently delighted them. Gail crept down to join them, and Nell turned with her finger over her lips while Kevin pointed silently downstairs.

The kitchen door was open just far enough for them to see Steve sitting on the bean bed, his head drooped in sleep, and Sammi curled blissfully in his arms.

CHAPTER EIGHT

ONCE the visit was under way Gail had expected to shut herself away with her word processor and leave Steve and his children together. But it didn't work out like that at all.

For one thing, there was Sammi. Gail liked dogs in any case, but between herself and Sammi it was love at first bite. The pup was about eight weeks old and strikingly beautiful, with long floppy ears. Her glossy coat was black, except for her paws, which had long white socks speckled with black, and the end of her tail, which looked as if it had been dipped in cream.

The first day Steve took the children out, Gail shut herself into the bedroom to try to come to terms with the machine. But Sammi, indignant at being excluded from the fun, created such uproar that Gail had to let her in and settle her on the bed with instructions to "Keep quiet," while she fought her way through the manual. With frequent interruptions she, the most unmechanical woman alive, got through the first lesson before deciding that they'd both earned a snack. Somehow a snack became a lively game in the garden, and when the family returned in the early evening they found Gail asleep on the bed, with Sammi beside her, contentedly shredding the manual.

They made a great game of her difficulties with the computer, and then Nell, who had a bent that way, showed her how it should be done. Steve joined in the laughter, and seemed cheerful enough, but Gail's acute wits detected an air of strain beneath the surface. And although she made a point of leaving the three of them alone, it seemed that Nell and Kevin actually preferred her to be there.

Nell had read *Drake Domino and the Scarlet Menace* and pronounced it first-rate. As Gail had half expected, the girl was instantly taken by the hero's wit and his way of disposing of his enemies with an elegant shrug. She was a bright child and found his methods of observation and deduction so appealing that she turned it into a game. Thereafter nobody was safe, from Sammi, who found herself convicted of having dug a hole in the flower bed on the evidence of a muddy nose, to Gail, who hadn't realised that she pulled her hair whenever a scene she was writing wouldn't come out right.

It was Nell who inadvertently revealed Gail's secret. She came into the bedroom one evening while Gail was working and Steve was sitting on the bed in his robe, doing a crossword puzzle. "I've brought you some tea," she said with suspicious innocence, setting down a small tray.

But the true reason for the visit became clear when they were sipping their tea and Nell lingered, trying to get a glimpse of what Gail was writing without seeming to do so. Gail smiled and went to sit on the bed to look over Steve's shoulder, pretending not to notice Nell. But Steve was less tactful. "What's so fascinating?" he asked his daughter.

Nell began to read aloud, "'Despite her resolve, Lady Madeline could no longer pretend that she was immune to Professor Savernake's demonic charm. The black glitter in his eyes seemed to hypnotise her, driving from her mind everything but his face with its great, noble forehead and high cheekbones. His dark hair swept back from—'" She stopped and giggled. "It sounds just like Daddy when he's cross."

"That's enough," Gail said hastily. "Give that to me. I don't like people reading my rough notes."

Nell handed the page over demurely. "Off to bed," Steve told her, grinning. When Nell had gone, he said nothing but looked at Gail with raised eyebrows.

"That child's imagination is too vivid," Gail observed coolly. "She's read something into it that isn't there."

"But I always knew I was your villain," he said, still grinning. "You cast me in the role that first evening in the restaurant."

"Oh, heck!"

"You have a very carrying voice. And when we were in the park, you said I'd been 'behaving like Professor Sav—' and then you stopped. I discovered who he was later when I dipped into your first book."

"You just happen to look the part," she said, trying to gather up her scattered dignity. "I use models wherever I can find them. I'd already written two books, remember. Mind you," she added fairly, "this one's easier now I've got a clear picture in my mind. I told you you'd been useful to me."

"I can see that I have. Well, it's nice to know. What other of my wicked characteristics have you drafted into service?"

"Steve, you are *not* Professor Savernake. You just happen to look like him."

He left it at that, and Gail breathed a sigh of relief that he hadn't apparently noticed anything else. But later that night, when they were lying side-by-side in the darkness, she felt the bed shake with his laughter. "Demonic charm, huh?"

"I was using my imagination," she said frostily.

"Sure you were."

"And it took a *lot* of imagination." She thought she heard a faint choke. "Oh, go to sleep," she told him, glad that he couldn't see her blushing in the darkness.

Gail found Nell both interesting and worrying, partly because she sensed that the little girl was like herself, a thinker whose head had to be engaged as well as her heart. At a time when she should have been enjoying the carefree pleasures of childhood, Nell was puzzling out the situation.

She began to find excuses to visit Gail, bringing her endless cups of tea and lingering. For the novelist in Gail these interruptions could be a strain. When her work was going well it tore her to shreds to be obliged to push it aside, but she forced herself to do so because she was aware that the child was slowly working around to something.

She encouraged Nell to talk about her life with the Kenleighs and found that she talked more easily about some things than others. She loved the agricultural shows where her grandparents had their moments of glory. "Grandpa has three dogs he enters for obedience trials," she said, "but Ella's the one who wins most prizes. She had four firsts last year. Grandpa says that's because she's a bitch and bitches are more intelligent than just plain dogs. She hasn't entered anything this year because she was having babies. She had five of them, and he says Sammi's the pick of the litter."

Hearing her name, the pup looked up from where she'd been chewing the carpet, but finding nothing of further interest she returned to her occupation.

"Grandpa sold all the others, and he was going to keep Sammi and train her for competitions, too," Nell went on, "but the day before we came here, Grandma said we could have her. They got terribly cross with each other."

"In front of you?" Gail asked, trying to sound casual.

Nell shook her head and looked a bit awkward. "I listened at the door," she confessed.

Gail gave her a reassuring smile. "I used to do a bit of that when I was a child," she said. "The grown-ups tell you it's wrong—well, it *is* wrong—but sometimes it's the only way to find out what's really going on."

Nell nodded with an expression of relief that uncannily mirrored her father's. "Especially with Grandma," she said.

Gail showed no special interest in this remark, but she was holding her breath. It was when she talked about Lady Kenleigh that Nell's confusion showed most. She loved her grandmother, but she wasn't blind to her methods. "Grandma says different things to different people," she said now, fiddling with the edge of the coverlet.

"What kind of things?" Gail asked gently.

"Well—" Nell wasn't looking at her. "When we were all here that evening, and you first said you were going to marry Daddy, she told you he was making use of you, and later I heard her telling Mr. Brace that—" She checked herself, embarrassed.

"I expect you heard her tell him that he only married me so that he could stay here," Gail said, helping her out.

Nell nodded gratefully. "She said he just wanted to 'make trouble.' But she told Kevin and me that Daddy hadn't really loved Mummy or he couldn't have married again so soon." She added reflectively, "I think she forgot that we were here the first time."

Gail's indignation at Lady Kenleigh's unscrupulous tactics was submerged in her alarm. She'd seen this problem coming and dreaded it. To let Nell believe Steve loved her would hurt the child. But to tell her the truth would risk her coming under Kenleigh pressure to reveal it. She crossed her fingers under the table and was about to embark on a careful answer when Nell exclaimed, "Sammi, you naughty girl! Look what you've done to the carpet!"

"It doesn't matter," Gail protested, but Nell had scooped the unrepentant culprit up into her arms.

"I'll take her away so that she can't bother you," she said, and vanished hurriedly. Gail sat in silence for a long time after that, wondering if she'd picked up Nell's signals correctly.

Later that night, when they were alone, she related the story to Steve. "How have you explained our marriage to them?" she asked him.

"I haven't. Like a coward, I've ducked it, and luckily they haven't asked."

"And they won't ask," she mused. "That's what Nell was telling me this afternoon. She knows some things are best left unsaid. It's terrible what that child understands that she shouldn't."

Steve scowled. "I should never have let Barbara bring them here."

"Well, perhaps it's not all Barbara's fault," Gail ventured.

"What's that supposed to mean?"

"I mean you should try to see things from their point of view. You may have broken with Barbara, but they didn't. She was their mother, and she's only been dead six months. You've no right to try to make them feel guilty because they still love her."

He stared at her for a long moment, then he rose abruptly and went to the drinks cabinet, poured himself a large whisky, downed it, poured another and returned to sit beside her at the sofa. His face was haggard, and now she realised that this look had been growing on it since the day his children had arrived. "Help me, Gail," he said desperately. "It's all going wrong, and I don't know why. For God's sake, help me!"

A terrible feeling of helplessness swept over Gail. It mattered so much to help Steve and see him happy. It was the most important thing in the world, and the sudden, shattering realisation of just how much his happiness mattered filled her with fear in case she failed him.

One small log burned in the fireplace against the evening chill. The flickering light emphasised the deep sockets of his eyes and the hollows in his lean cheeks, but for once Gail didn't think of Professor Savernake. She only thought how tired and sad Steve looked and how it would feel to pull his head down to her breast and comfort him. How wonderful to hold him against her, not in passion but in tenderness, and tell him that she loved him.

It was easy to see now that she'd loved him since the first evening, not from the moment he'd kissed her, but from when she'd seen his face as he held his children against his heart. She'd rationalised the emotions that had seized her then, telling herself she was too susceptible to the sight of father love. But now they wouldn't be rationalised anymore. They dominated her thoughts when he was absent and her senses when he was near, and they demanded to be recognised for what they were, love for the man himself.

But he didn't love her. He'd been at pains to make that clear. She could call herself his friend, but no more. And now he was imploring her help as a friend, and she loved him enough to put self aside and give him the comfort he needed, free of emotional pressure. "Tell me what's happened," she said. "I've noticed the three of you never seem very relaxed with each other when you come home."

"I think we're all equally glad to get back to you," Steve said, "so that we can stop looking at each other in dismay because we have nothing to talk about. I don't understand it. We were never stuck for words when we met before."

"Perhaps that's because you met under such strained conditions," Gail suggested. "Every meeting was a victory over the people who were trying to keep you apart."

"Yes," he agreed heavily. "And now we don't have the battle to talk about, we have nothing else in common. We don't know each other anymore, and I'm not even sure they *want* to know me. All this time I've gone on believing that we had a bond nothing could destroy. On my side that's true, but they—" he broke off and drew a painful breath. "I see them looking at me like strangers, and I'm terrified that when the time comes they'll say they want to stay here."

"Steve, I don't believe that. You're their father, and they love you."

"I wonder. Do you know what scares me most, Gail? It's that they've started being dreadfully polite to me in a kind of frozen way."

"That's only because they're trying not to say the wrong thing."

"If they felt close to me there would be no 'wrong thing.' They can talk to you. Why not me?"

"I suppose I'm the only person who isn't fighting to win them over, so they can relax and tell me their real thoughts and feelings."

"But why *shouldn't* they tell me their real feelings?"

"Because you wouldn't like to hear them," Gail said simply. "You don't like people feeling differently from you, Steve, and you get hostile when they refuse you what you want. In your book, Barbara and her parents are monsters, but your children don't see them that way."

"And they're scared to say that? Are you saying my children are afraid of me?"

"No, but they're afraid of hurting you, Nell especially." Gail hesitated before adding gently, "She knows you can't take very much."

Steve turned startled eyes towards her. Then he slumped back into his seat. "Is that really true?" he asked.

Gail was silent, trying to find the courage for the most painful decision in her life. Steve had begged her to help him win back his children's love, because that meant more to him than anything else on earth. But now she knew that to give him his heart's desire she must reconcile him with Barbara and make him remember that he'd once loved her. And if, in the process, she broke her own heart, that was nobody's problem but hers.

She looked at him sitting in the gently flickering light, read the despair on his face and knew that he was worth suffering for. "Steve, listen to me," she said earnestly, sliding down so that she was sitting on the floor looking up at him.

"I'll listen," he said. "You're the only one who seems to have any of the answers."

"Nell and Kevin are marvellous kids. They're loving and intelligent, strong and kind. I think you must be a wonderful man to produce children like that." From this angle she could hardly see his face at all, but she had the impression that he'd grown even more still. She went on, speaking carefully, feeling her way by inches over this dangerous territory. "But that also means—doesn't it?—that Barbara must have been a wonderful woman."

He stared at her. "Gail, whose side are you on?"

"Theirs," she said without hesitation. "Nell's and Kevin's. Don't you realise that they're watching you and waiting for you to give them what they need, and if you fail them, they'll never forgive you?"

"What is it they need? Tell me, Gail."

"Your permission to grieve for their mother," she said quietly.

She felt his convulsive jerk and knew she'd taken a risk, but she'd deliberately put it in the starkest possible terms. Time was running out.

"Do you know what a terrible thing you've just said?" Steve asked in a low voice.

"No more terrible than what's happening to your children. I don't know what kind of a wife Barbara was, but I think she was probably a delightful mother with a

lot of simplicity in her nature that children could relate
to. They loved her, and she's only been dead six months.
They need to talk their grief out.''

''The Kenleighs—''

''I don't suppose they can discuss Barbara with them.
From what Nell's let drop, I think she's tried, but Lady
Kenleigh takes it as a chance to put more emotional
pressure on them. You know the kind of thing, 'If you
loved Mummy you'd prove it by staying with Grandma.'
Perhaps not actually in those words, but you don't need
to spell things out to Nell, and Kevin follows where she
leads.

''They need to talk to *you* and they can't do that as
long as they know you're hostile to Barbara. You love
them, but you're forcing them to choose between loving you and loving their mother's memory.''

''Oh, God!'' he said, and dropped his head into his
hands.

She touched his hair gently, and at once he twined his
fingers in hers as though he was holding on to his only
safety. ''Tell me what to do,'' he pleaded.

''You have to try to remember.''

Steve looked up. ''I don't understand.''

''You've got to remember Barbara and how much
you once loved her. Try to see her again as you did
then.''

''But how can I?'' he demanded in despair. ''You've
said yourself I'm no good at seeing through someone
else's eyes.''

''Not someone else's, your own, as you once were.
Remember what you told me about the day you first
saw her, how she laughed as she took the fall and how
attractive you found that?''

Slowly Steve leaned back and looked into the distance, seeming to see pictures there. "She never lost her smile on a horse," he said. "When she got up she waved at the crowd and then she patted the horse's neck to reassure him. She never blamed an animal for what might have been her own mistake."

"Because she was generous and kind," Gail urged. As she saw his mouth twist wryly, she hurried on, "Yes, she was, Steve. When she was in her true element she was always good-natured, wasn't she?"

There was a long silence before Steve said heavily, "Yes, she was. I'd forgotten that, but it was true. When I first knew her, she was always finding excuses for people. She could never believe that anyone had acted out of meanness or spite or dishonesty. She'd say they must have a headache or be worried about something. She had a sunny nature."

"And when you were just married, living from hand to mouth, how was she then?"

"Marvellous. She'd always had everything she wanted, and suddenly there was very little money, but she made light of it. She said nothing mattered as long as we were together."

Gail was glad he couldn't see her face. It would reveal more than he must ever know. She dug her nails into her palm before her next question, trying to counter the pain of what she was doing to herself. "When she was so nice about it, how did that make you feel about her?" she asked.

She dug her nails in harder as she heard his voice soften. "I though she was wonderful, so brave and funny. She never blamed me for taking her away from luxury, can you imagine that?"

Sitting on the floor beside him in the near darkness Gail thought, *Yes, I can imagine it. I'd care nothing for poverty, either, if we were together, if it were the thought of me that brought that gentle, wondering note to your voice.*

"But I blamed myself," Steve went on. "I hated myself when I saw her go without because... because it made me think her mother had been right, that I'd snatched her away from the world where she belonged through my own pride and arrogance. I felt so guilty." There was a long, tense silence before Steve added quietly, "I guess I'm not a very nice person when I feel guilty."

He didn't say any more for a while. Gail sat in silence, uncomfortably aware of the loud beating of her heart. At last he continued, "We began to fight. Even when things went better, the arguments continued. I could give her nice things then, but she didn't seem to want them. She hated my work and everything it paid for. Once, she accused me of trying to buy her off. That hurt, because all I wanted was to see her smile—but she never seemed to smile anymore.

"Even the children came between us sometimes. I adored them, and I thought they'd bring us together, but she was very possessive about them. I think I see why, now." He laid a hand on Gail's shoulder, as if needing her to confirm his thoughts. "She felt they were all she had, didn't she?"

She took his hand in a friendly clasp. "I think so. I don't believe Barbara ever stopped loving you for a moment, or—or that you stopped loving her."

Gail wasn't sure he'd heard her. His eyes were closed, and he was talking half to himself. "I should have tried to understand her, but I'd always succeeded by barging my way through difficulties, and I couldn't see that this was different. I see it now, but it's too late.''

Gail didn't know what made her look up just then. But she did, and in the dim light of the doorway she could just make out two small figures, very still, listening. She hardly breathed.

''I left her stranded, didn't I?'' Steve said in a voice of discovery. ''Once, we were everything to each other, but she died not knowing how much she mattered to me. I wasn't even there to ask her to forgive me. And now it's too late, and I wish—''

The two figures had been creeping forward slowly and were very close now, waiting for something that had yet to happen. Then a slight sound made Steve open his eyes. He made an inarticulate noise and opened his arms, and they flung themselves into them.

Gail rose quietly and went to the door. She turned and stood for a moment, looking at Steve's children clinging to him eagerly. She saw him drop his head so that it was resting on Nell's, saw the glint of tears, although whose they were she couldn't tell. Then she slipped away.

She wasn't sure if any of the three who'd found each other at last knew that she'd gone. The only thing she was quite sure of was that none of them needed her anymore.

CHAPTER NINE

THE next day Gail remained alone in the house to work while Steve and the children went out. She was just getting into her stride when she heard Lady Kenleigh calling from below, "Is anyone here?"

She was in the living room, having simply walked in through the French doors. Gail wondered how long she'd been looking around. But she suppressed her annoyance and greeted her pleasantly. Lady Kenleigh was holding a small blanket. She smiled, and at once Gail knew that she was less confident than she seemed. "I only came to bring this," she said. "It's Samantha's. The children forgot it."

The excuse was so blatant and pathetic that Gail felt a twinge of pity. "Thank you," she said. "Steve and the children have gone out, but why don't we have some tea together?"

She led the way into the kitchen with its view over the rear lawn, where Sammi was bouncing about, uttering terrible threats to a twig. Lady Kenleigh watched for a moment. "She seems well and happy," she observed. "I'm so glad. Sometimes, when a pup's just been taken from its mother, it can't settle, and I just thought... since I was passing..." She was talking too fast, and her eyes were desperate.

"You dropped in to make sure she was all right," Gail said, smiling. She wasn't taken in, but it seemed kinder to pretend. "That was nice of you."

Gail made tea, and they took it into the living room. "How are—how are you all?" Lady Kenleigh asked.

"We're all fine. Steve and the children are really happy to be seeing something of each other again."

"I believe you said they were out?" Lady Kenleigh asked, a little too casually.

"Yes." Gail hesitated before saying gently, "They're visiting his wife's grave together. Steve wanted to put some flowers on it."

A dreadful look of despair settled over the old woman's face.

She knows, Gail thought. *Now Steve's reconciled with Barbara's memory, the children have turned towards him. She knows she's lost.*

Then Lady Kenleigh's lips curved in a small, cold smile. "His wife. Yes, *she* really was his wife." Gail said nothing, refusing to be provoked. She pitied this sad, embittered woman, and a moment later she knew she'd been right, for Lady's Kenleigh's austere expression relaxed and she said tiredly, "I'm sorry. That was very rude."

"I didn't take offence," Gail assured her. "I know you're unhappy."

She half expected to be snubbed, but the older woman simply closed her eyes and nodded. "What made him want to see her grave today?" she asked.

"He's been doing some thinking," Gail said carefully, "and they've talked a lot about Barbara. He found he wasn't as hostile to her as he'd thought."

Something in her voice made Lady Kenleigh say wryly, "You think I deliberately fostered that, don't you?"

"I think you'd use any weapon you found at hand," Gail said frankly.

Lady Kenleigh smiled wryly. "Well, of course, I would, I'm not a fool." She gave Gail an appraising glance and said unexpectedly, "You're not, either. It's strange. If I lose, it'll be thanks to you, I know that. But if we'd met in a different way I know I could say things to you that no one else would understand."

"Why don't you try me?" Gail offered. "I'm not your enemy, and I don't think you have many people you can confide in."

"I don't have anyone," the older woman said simply. "I'm all alone in this, and nobody understands." Her voice wobbled on the last words, but she regained control. "I've always been alone, and I always will be."

"What about your husband?" Gail ventured.

"Him?" Lady Kenleigh's voice was scathing. "He doesn't care about anything but his dogs. Oh, he loved Barbara in his own way. He loved *me* once in his own way, but... I don't know... he's always been happier with dogs than people."

Gail nodded. "Some people are like that. They find animals easier to relate to."

Lady Kenleigh spoke with the bewilderment of forty years. "But it doesn't make any sense."

"It does if a man isn't very sure of himself," Gail said sympathetically. "Dogs are less demanding than people. They let you make the rules and don't talk back."

"Yes, William never *did* like arguments." Lady Kenleigh sighed. "Not that he ever got angry. He just slipped away to the kennels. It was so maddening trying to make him listen."

Gail privately thought that any diffidence in Sir William had probably been exacerbated by his wife's masterful nature, but she wasn't unkind enough to say so. If there was one chance in a million that she could win this prickly woman's confidence, she must seize it. It might be the last and most vital service she could perform for the man she loved.

"But then I had Barbara," Lady Kenleigh said in a voice that was suddenly softer. "And I wasn't alone anymore. If you knew how much I looked forward to her growing up and being a companion to me. Of course, I knew she'd get married, but there were so many nice young men of her own kind around here. I thought everything would still be much the same afterward, and it could have been ...

"But then he came here, and he wanted to take my lovely girl three thousand miles away, where I'd never see her. I used to pray every night for him to go away or for her to see through him, but it was no use. She ran off with him, and I didn't even know she was gone until it was too late. She rang me from Boston, and it was too late, *too late...*."

Lady Kenleigh dropped her head into her hands and cried. Shocked by so much anguish, Gail laid a hand on her shoulder, and Lady Kenleigh reached out blindly and clutched it. "She was all I had," she sobbed, "and he took her away from me." At last she raised a ravaged face. "Don't you see, she was mine? I had every right to take her back."

Gail shook her head and spoke as kindly as she could. "But we can't own people. Sometimes—" a tremor shook her but she forced herself to go on "—sometimes we have to let them go if it's best for them—"

"But it *wasn't* best for her. When she brought the children home to visit me that time, I knew she wasn't happy. And she soon saw that she really belonged with her own kind."

"So you persuaded her to stay here?"

"Yes," Lady Kenleigh said with a kind of bitter triumph. "She called him to say she wasn't going back, just as she'd done with me."

Her victory was so blinkered, so selfish and so pitiful that Gail could find nothing to say.

"I thought everything would be lovely, just as it used to be," Lady Kenleigh continued, "but then she died. The children are all I have left of her, and he wants to take them away, too. Don't you understand? Once he's taken them back to America, I'll never see them again."

"I think that depends on you," Gail said thoughtfully. "I don't think you can win now, and if you fight to the bitter end you probably *will* be excluded. But Nell and Kevin don't want to be fought over. They want a united family, and it's up to you and Steve to give it to them."

Lady Kenleigh looked at her oddly. "Have you said all this to him?"

"Yes, I have. If you let the children go, you'll keep their love, and if *they* want to see you again, I think Steve will invite you."

The other woman gave a short, disbelieving laugh. "I don't think that's very likely. I suppose he told you to say all this—get round the old woman and make her give in. What can you know about my grandchildren?"

"I know they need love, both yours and his. Can't you let them go with him without any more fighting? I don't think you'll ever regret it."

Lady Kenleigh's face was a mask of bitterness. "You're as clever at persuasion as he's bad at it. Oh, he really knew what he was doing when he got you on his side."

Gail sighed. Anguish had made Lady Kenleigh harden her heart, and there seemed no way through to her. "I'm sorry you feel that way," she said.

Lady Kenleigh rose to her feet and said, "There's nothing more for us to say. I'd better go." Faithful to a lifetime's training she added politely, "Thank you very much for the tea."

Gail watched her go in despair. She'd had her chance, and she'd blown it.

She went back to the book and tried to concentrate. Steve's troubles had taken up so much of her time that she'd done very little work since the wedding. But she found it hard to focus on her characters when her thoughts kept wandering to the quiet little country churchyard where a father and his children were putting flowers on a grave.

At midday the phone rang. It was Steve. "Just to say we'll be late coming home," he said. "We're going for a drive."

"Thanks for letting me know."

"Are you all right. You sound a bit funny."

"No, I'm just frazzled."

"Drake Domino being a pain in the neck?"

"Yes, as always," she said brightly.

"You'll be glad to have us out of the way, then. We'll eat out so we won't bother you."

"Is everything all right?"

His voice grew softer. "Everything's wonderful, Gail. We're really talking to each other again and— Okay, Kevin, I'm coming. I'd better go. The kids are getting impatient."

"Do you have any idea when you'll be back," she asked desperately.

"None at all. Probably late. Bye." He hung up.

Gail replaced the receiver, wondering where was the joy she should be feeling. She'd worked to bring this about, and it had gone better than she'd dared to hope. They would probably drive out into the country, somewhere quiet where they could talk about Barbara. Memories would come flooding back, and Steve's feelings would revive even more. Gail closed her eyes and wished it were as easy to close her heart to the pain of being no longer wanted.

They returned in the early evening. The children were sleepy but happy, and Gail noticed how they instinctively stood closer to their father than before and turned to him with smiling eagerness. It was Steve who got them a light supper and put them to bed, telling Gail that he didn't want to disturb her work. But she couldn't dismiss the feeling that all three of them preferred to be without her. That feeling was reinforced when Steve stayed talking in their room for a long time. Gail could hear the murmur of voices through the thin wall connecting their room with hers. The longing to try to catch the words was terrible, and at last she went downstairs to save herself from temptation.

When Steve came down later, she was stretched on the sofa, listening to a quietly playing record and trying to make the tension leave her. He poured her a sherry and himself a whisky and settled on a low seat beside her. "Tired?" he said sympathetically.

"A bit."

"Poor Gail. We've been a burden on you, but that's all over, I promise."

"You haven't been a burden, Steve, any of you."

Smiling, he leaned over and dropped a light kiss on her lips, but didn't follow it up. His face was aglow with happiness. "You've never complained, but from now on, it's going to be just as we agreed."

She smiled, wishing he would stop. "I'm glad it worked out for you," she said.

"Worked out? I can't find words to tell you—"

"Then don't try," she said quickly. "There are some things you just can't describe."

"But I must," he said eagerly, "because it was you who brought it all about."

"All right," she said in a colourless voice.

"We went to buy some flowers, and the strangest thing happened. I suddenly remembered that Barbara liked yellow chrysanthemums, although I hadn't thought of it for years. So I bought some, and we went to lay them on her grave. I'd been there before, but this was different. We were together—I mean *really* together—not just physically but—"

Gail smiled. "It's all right, I understand what you're saying."

"Of course, you do. I don't have to explain things to you. And when we got to the grave...Kevin took my hand. I can't remember the last time he did that. He's just getting to the age when boys think it's unmanly, but he held my hand tightly. And he didn't try to hide the fact that he was crying."

"That's wonderful," Gail said, meaning it. "What about Nell?"

"I'm not sure what to make of Nell. She's a strange, quiet little thing. Luckily she seems fairly sturdy, not as vulnerable as Kevin."

"But she is," Gail said urgently. "Steve, don't ever think that Nell doesn't need you just because she seems more independent. She's far too wise for her age, and she has a way of noticing things that could be dangerous, because she doesn't always talk about what she's seen, just broods on her own.''

"All right, I'll remember. Anyway, I know she feels she can talk to you."

"Yes, but..." Gail couldn't bring herself to go any further. This wasn't the time to put into words her dread that the parting might be nearer than they'd expected.

"Come to think of it, I know what you mean about noticing," Steve said suddenly. "After we left the churchyard, Nell asked me why I'd chosen those particular flowers, and I got a funny feeling, as if she was testing me to see if I'd really remembered or if it was an accident." He saw Gail nodding and said, a little self-consciously, "Thanks to you I'm beginning to get it right."

Gail shook her head. "You can get it right without me, now you've found the key. How did you answer her?"

"I told them how Mummy had once said she liked yellow chrysanthemums because they were so cheerful, and how I'd thought they suited her because she was such a cheerful person herself. I said I'd bought her some on the day we met. And then Nell—" He stopped, then said with a sigh, "I feel bad because I never knew this, but Barbara had kept one. Nell found it pressed in a book after she died, with the date. She must have done it that evening, but she left her books behind when we ran away. It's strange really...."

"What is?" Gail prompted.

"You'd have thought she'd have thrown it out when she left me. But perhaps she'd forgotten about it."

"Or perhaps she still loved you?"

Gail wished she knew how to interpret the look on Steve's face. He was uneasy, but did that spring from a reluctance to admit the truth to her? Was it regret for a past that could never be recaptured? "I'll never know," he said at last.

"I don't think she wanted to leave you, and she wouldn't have done if her mother hadn't urged her."

"I always wondered if Cornelia—" He stopped and stared at her. "How do you know that?"

"Lady Kenleigh told me. She was here today." She related the conversation and added, "She was set on getting Barbara back and put a lot of pressure on her. But for that—" she forced herself to go on "—I don't think she'd have left you. She'd have come back and worked your problems out, because she still loved you, Steve."

"You seem very sure of that," he said quietly.

It was easy to be sure because the depth of her own love gave her insight into Barbara's heart, but she only said, "It's pretty obvious, isn't it?"

"I wish it was obvious to me. Why are you so set on convincing me, now that it's too late?"

"It's not too late for Nell and Kevin. I'm glad you bought those yellow chrysanthemums."

He looked at her strangely for a long moment before saying, "You really *are* glad, aren't you?"

"With all my heart," she said firmly. "Steve, there's something I haven't told you yet. I told Lady Kenleigh that if she let you have Nell and Kevin, you'd let her visit them in Boston whenever she wanted."

"The hell I will!" he growled. "The less they see of her the better."

"Then you'll hurt them again. They love her, too."

Steve's face had a dark look that showed how far he still had to travel before he could accept this. Gail tried again, using all the emotional force at her command.

"She's not a monster, Steve, just a very unhappy, lonely old woman. I don't think Sir William is much use as a husband. She opposed you years ago because she was terrified of being left alone, and now she's terrified again. You must give her some hope to cling on to."

He regarded her keenly. "And if I do that, she'll give in?"

Gail sighed, "No, she didn't say that but—"

"And she won't. Bless you for trying, Gail, but I know Cornelia Kenleigh better than you do. She won't budge an inch, and I don't want my children under her influence one moment longer than can be helped."

"But if she *did* give in—you wouldn't make me out a liar, would you?"

His face wore a hard, stubborn look. "There's no point in talking about it. It simply isn't going to happen."

Gail came into her room a few days later to find Nell stretched out on her bed, so absorbed in a book that at first she didn't hear anything. When she realised she wasn't alone she looked up with a start. "I just—you have such lovely books."

"You can read them whenever you like," Gail said, smiling. "What have you got there? The poems of John Donne?" She was startled as she read the name of the sixteenth-century intellectual. "Can you understand them?" she said, looking at Nell curiously.

"Some of them, a bit. The love poems are terribly unkind. He never seems to think people are going to love each other for long." Nell pointed to the open page. "He starts this one saying, 'Now thou hast loved me one whole day,' and you can tell he thinks that's a lot. Then he lists all the excuses she'll make when she's tired of him and says he won't bother to contradict her because he'll probably be tired of her, as well.''

Gail laughed, but she was feeling uneasy. She'd learned that Nell seldom talked for the sake of it. Whatever she said had an underlying meaning, and there was something ominous in her reading poems about the fragility of love. ''And there's this one,'' Nell went on, flicking over pages until she came to ''A Lecture upon the Shadow.'' ''He says the shadows of morning are like when people first fall in love, and they pretend it isn't happening because they're afraid, but gradually the shadows vanish.''

''And midday is the moment when love is perfect, because there are no shadows,'' Gail said, studying the page. ''That's rather lovely.''

''Yes, but he says that then new shadows start and everything goes wrong, until finally it's all darkness.'' She read aloud:

> The morning shadows wear away, But these grow longer all the day, But oh, love's day is short, if love decay. Love is a growing or full constant light; And his first minute after noon, is night.

Gail knew that now it mattered to choose the right words as it had never mattered before. Nell had seen her parents' love turn into night, and now she thought all love ended like that. She might grow up never knowing how to find love, because she couldn't believe in it. ''It doesn't always happen like that,'' Gail said urgently. ''Some people do find the 'full constant light' that shines all their lives. Donne found it himself. After all his cynical talk, he married a woman he was terribly in love with and adored her all the years of their marriage.''

"But Mummy and Daddy weren't like that, were they?"

"Your parents were unlucky," Gail said. "They were very young, and they had a lot against them. But they loved each other. Sometimes—sometimes love shows itself in ways that we don't understand."

She sent the child away looking happier and stayed behind brooding on the poem herself. With a true instinct, Nell had likened the shadows of morning to falling in love. The girl's words, "...when people first fall in love, and they pretend it isn't happening because they're afraid," haunted her.

She was no longer pretending to herself that she wasn't in love with Steve, but it would be a long time before she could drop the pretence with him. Perhaps she could never drop it, and her love would turn to night without ever having reached its zenith.

Or perhaps in time she would win his love, and they could live in the full constant light. But for that she needed time, and she didn't know how much time might be left.

CHAPTER TEN

GAIL had fallen into the routine of working in the evening after the children had gone to bed and Steve was downstairs making calls. At about eleven he would come up, assuring her that he could sleep through anything and she was free to continue working. Then he would bury himself under the covers and be dead to the world. When she crept in beside him a couple of hours later, he never moved or gave any sign of knowing that she was there. In this way they got through the nights together, side-by-side in the double bed. Her late hours would often cause her to oversleep, and she usually awoke to find herself alone.

As she wrestled with the book's climax, Gail's problems multiplied. The great confrontation between the elegant aristocrat and his wily opponent refused to come out right, for which Professor Savernake was entirely to blame. Instead of lying down and admitting defeat when his creator told him to, he kept reminding her that his Machiavellian cunning would get him out of anything Drake Domino could think up. Besides which, he was at least as charming and intriguing as the hero and deserved to fight another day. Gail, who'd been toying with the idea of disposing of him completely, was forced to sit by and watch him take over.

One night he was being particularly troublesome. The back of Gail's neck was aching and her fingers had typed so much that they were beginning to feel numb. She yawned and stretched, knowing she must get out of the house for some fresh air before she could do any more. As she went downstairs, she could hear Steve on the phone. She slipped out without disturbing him.

The night air was blessedly cool, and she stood for a moment, drinking it in, before wandering around the corner of the cottage to where there were a few trees. A brilliant moon cast a sheen of silver over the surfaces, making the hollows twice as black. The cottage stood on a small incline, and from here she could see the outskirts of Chalmley to her left, while to her right there was the countryside stretching away into the distance. Everything was very quiet.

The ground was dry, and she settled down on it, looking up into the sky where a few small clouds drifted and the dazzling moon flooded even the clouds with light. She thought sleepily how lovely it would be if everything could stop here and she could float on with the moon into infinity.

She seemed to hear her own name, but it came from a long way away, and it disturbed the warm haziness that was beginning to envelope her, so she tried to ignore the sound. But it came again, louder.

She didn't move. If she stayed still and quiet she could reach up and become the moon, free of all cares, free. . . .

"Gail, are you there?" Steve was crossing the lawn, looking around him, approaching the trees. "Is that you?"

She had an exhilarating feeling of light-headedness that made her laugh and say, "No."

"It sounds like you." He came closer. "Where are you? It's so dark here."

He approached, moving carefully. Outside the pool of shadow everything was dazzling silver, but within it the darkness was so black it seemed to swallow all light. He peered, vainly trying to see her. "Gail?"

She reached up to him, cutting across the boundary of the shadow, so that her shimmering white hand seemed to float, disembodied, against the night. "Are you a ghost?" he asked, smiling.

"Not a ghost," she said dreamily, "the moon."

He took her hand and let her guide him down. Gail felt him settle close to her and breathed in the pleasantly nutty aroma he always carried with him. It mingled with the scents of the earth that rose around her into the warm night air, making her senses reel and her hold on reality loosen. "Did I hear you right?" Steve asked. "I thought you said you were the moon."

"I did." She pointed up to the glimmering orb above them. "Isn't she beautiful? It's the perfect night for being the moon."

"You haven't gotten into the sherry, have you?" he asked cautiously.

She chuckled softly, and it seemed to invade him like magic, running through his veins until he was enchanted, too. "Yes, I think I must be drunk," she said, "but not with sherry."

"With words?"

"With words and dreams," she mused. "It's like drinking nectar."

"And it turns you into the moon?" he said, catching her mood.

"It turns me into whatever I want. If I think hard enough I can be anything in the world—the moon, the sea, the stars, the wind."

In the darkness he could just make out the faint glow of her face, and he peered closer, trying to see her eyes. He'd known Gail when she was indignant, practical, funny and bossy. He'd known her cold with fury and burning with passion, her slim eager body aglow in his arms, inciting his blood to riot. But this was the first time he'd known her whimsical. Now he discovered her power to leave the earth behind and take a flight into fantasy, and he felt a wild longing to put his hand in hers and beg her to let him fly with her.

But he was earthbound, and he felt the frustration of knowing that only her body was there. Her heart and soul had soared away to regions where he couldn't follow. "And tonight you want to be the moon?" he said, gamely clinging to the shimmering wake that streamed behind her. "Why?"

"Because she's free. Nothing touches her serenity, no old ghosts haunt her—she's just here and now with no tomorrow to worry about."

He sighed at the thought of a life where there was no tomorrow and, therefore, no fear, where he could open his arms to his children without dreading the judge who might take them away. And perhaps, too, he could open his arms to her, and she would look at him and really see him at last. "What would you do if there was no tomorrow?" he whispered.

She didn't answer, but he heard a slight rustle as her head turned, and he knew she was looking up at him. He suddenly felt he had to see her expression, and he pulled her up into a sitting position. But the pale, moonlit face he saw belonged to someone he didn't know. This wasn't Gail, but a creature from another world, half woman, half spirit, and totally alluring. He felt her hand slide over his cheek into his hair, pulling him down to her. He saw a mysterious smile play about her mouth and dared to touch it with his own. He whispered, "Moon, where are you leading me?"

"Does it matter?" she whispered back.

Did it matter? He'd been trying, ever since they'd met, to find the key to Gail, but he was still baffled. Her gift for being all things to all people had been at first a delight and then a maddening frustration as he felt himself falling in love with her. It was impossible to speak of his feelings when he never knew which woman he was talking to.

At Brighton he'd been almost overcome with desire for her, until the news from Leonard had recalled him to his true purpose, making him ashamed of how totally he'd forgotten it in her company. Gail herself had provided the next reminder, taking charge of the court-room negotiations in a businesslike fashion. After that he'd backed off, knowing how much he needed her friendship to recover his children and fearful of jeopardising that friendship by seeking more.

He'd been alert for her signals, watching for any sign that she wanted him. But she'd devoted herself to reconciling him with Barbara, saying things that no woman who loved him could have said. He'd realised, with dismay, that her ability to enter into others' feelings was no more than a writer's knack. Her generosity and sympathy didn't mean that she cared for him personally.

He'd been angry with her. What right did she have to play havoc with his heart while remaining so cool herself? But the anger had passed. He couldn't live close to her without hoping.

Tonight he'd felt his hopes being fulfilled. She'd reached out and pulled him down to her. Once again she'd left him wondering who she was, yet somehow that was no longer important. The only thing that counted was that they were in each other's arms. "Take me with you," he whispered.

"I'll take you," she murmured. "There's nowhere we can't go."

She put her soul into the kiss she gave him. She loved him so much, and she could only tell him like this, when they weren't completely themselves. Her lips couldn't frame the words, but they could touch his again and again and hope he understood. His own mouth was warm and firm, and it answered the caresses of hers with skill and ardour.

She felt the tip of his tongue tracing the curved outline of her lips, a soft, delicate touch that tantalised her. She let her lips part, willing him to invade her, and she gave a sigh of pleasure as his tongue began to explore the inside of her mouth gently, evoking magical sensations wherever it flickered against the silky surface.

Her tongue was in his mouth, teasing him, rejoicing in the reaction she could feel. She was making love with the man she loved, and she knew now that he couldn't resist her. She slid her fingers down from where they were wound in his hair, playing on the back of his neck, and felt the tremors of delight go through him. Emboldened, she caressed him further, tracing the line of his jaw with her fingertips, feeling the strong column of his neck tense under her loving provocation.

She heard him whisper, "The moon's an enchantress," as he held her close and began to rain kisses along the line of her jaw, then down her neck. She hadn't known the hollow of her throat was so sensitive until Steve placed his lips there, but that gentle caressing touch sent her into a spiral of delight. She wanted him to kiss her everywhere, and he seemed to know it because he was easing open the buttons of her shirt. He moved slowly, but she was wild with impatience and pulled the last few buttons open for him.

She felt, rather than heard him sigh as though she'd told him something he was waiting to know, then he moved swiftly, rising to his feet and drawing her up with him.

They made their way upstairs in darkness. In their room he took her into his arms and kissed her with tender passion, gently easing her shirt off without taking his mouth from hers. Neither knew which of them drew the other down to the bed, but they were lying together, and his lips were on her breast. She arched up against him in ecstasy. She wanted him in every way a woman could want a man, and now the power of fantasy had freed them from their daily selves, for one magic night he could be hers alone.

The moonlight streamed in, and when they'd discarded their clothes they lay together, their limbs entwined, bathed in silver light. He looked down at her and ran reverent hands over her body, tracing the curves and hollows with joyful wonder. He wanted to whisper her name, but feared to do so in case it broke the spell.

Gail felt as if she were dissolving into another dimension. Her love overwhelmed her, blotting out everything but joy in what was happening and her fierce resolve to claim him fully. Tonight everything was beautiful, from the tenderness with which Steve sought her and caressed her intimately, to the passion that flowed like a current between their bodies, so that neither could have said where one ended and the other began. The rapture of their union was heart stopping in its intensity. And when it was over, it wasn't really over at all, because she still felt a part of him, just as he was a part of her, and would be forever.

They made love again, coming to meet each other with mounting desire, knowing each other now, taking and giving as though they'd been made for this and had been waiting all their lives. The pleasure was almost frightening, but greater than pleasure was the joy of being one with him at last.

Gail held him to her afterward, his head pillowed on her breast, listening to his breathing become slower. She'd had her moment of love fulfilled, and just now she wouldn't look ahead or ask if the future held other moments or only sadness. For the moon, there was no tomorrow.

Gail awoke and lay for a long moment, seeing the brilliant light of morning through her eyelids but refusing to open them. She wanted to deny the daylight and cling on a little longer to the magic night that had passed. In the darkness she and Steve had found each other, and the discovery had been wonderful. She'd given him everything she had of heart and body, and what she'd received in return even she, who was skilled with words, could never describe. Surely now the moment had come when they could acknowledge the truth they'd been concealing and turn to each other as true lovers.

She opened her eyes at last and looked at the clock. She'd slept late, but now she was rapidly waking up, with a sense of well-being that started deep inside the body that could only ever be his.

She heard laughter outside and, pulling on a robe, went to the window to see Steve and the children kicking a ball around, with Sammi making an eager fourth. She pushed open the window and laughed. The noise attracted Steve, who looked up. "'Morning," he called cheerfully. "I'm sorry if we woke you."

"You didn't. I'd have woken anyway."

"Good. Sleep all right?"

"Fine, thank you."

"You were dead to the world when I—*Nell*, get that dog off the flower bed. This garden isn't ours."

Gail watched the mad scramble in the garden below with eyes that didn't see. A chill had invaded her at Steve's comradely tone.

Down below, the game had resumed. Gail drew back inside and went to have a shower. There was nothing to wait for. She knew now that Steve wouldn't come hurrying upstairs to take her in his arms. He wouldn't look into her eyes, seeking reassurance that the night had meant the same to her as to him. Had it meant anything to him at all?

Steve saw her appear in the kitchen half an hour later and knew that he must go in and speak to her. He shrank from it because the next few minutes would be the most vital of his life, and he knew he was going to handle them badly. His confidence, once so overmastering, had shrunk. Gail had shown him how his habit of being so bullheaded hurt those he loved, and he was still raw from the fresh look she'd given him at his marriage. Fear seized him that he was going to make the same mistakes again and drive away the woman he most wanted to cling to.

He delayed until it couldn't be put off any longer, then went into the kitchen. She looked up from pouring coffee and gave him the briefest smile. "That coffee smells wonderful. I'll have some, please," he said.

She was wearing old jeans and a check shirt, and with her golden skin and fair hair she looked like a fresh country lass, down-to-earth and completely different from the fey creature he'd held in his arms the previous night. This change of character unnerved him still further, and the words he'd been planning to say went out of his head. "You look well this morning," he said lamely.

"All I needed was a good rest."

"Yes. You were—not quite yourself last night."

I was myself for the first time last night, she thought.

She shrugged. "I get those idiotic moods sometimes. I'm sorry if I alarmed you."

She'd lain in his arms like the embodiment of beauty, holding him spellbound with the warmth and wonder of her love—or so he'd thought. Now he heard how it had seemed to her. *"Those idiotic moods."*

"I wasn't so much alarmed as bewildered." He laughed awkwardly. "I never really know where I am with you, Gail. You seem to produce a new rabbit out of the hat for every situation. It confuses a man."

Gail poured herself another coffee, keeping her face averted from him. "And which rabbit did I produce last night?" she asked, sounding only amused.

He matched her tone. "You had some crazy idea about being the moon. Don't you remember?"

"How can I?" she said lightly. "The moon has no tomorrow." She furrowed her forehead as though trying to recall an obscure detail. "Didn't we say that?"

He smiled to cover his pain. "Right," he said too heartily. "Well, that's what I mean, I don't want you to think I read anything into it. We can go on as if nothing happened, if we like."

He put the faintest emphasis on the final three words, trusting her to notice and understand that he was asking what *she* liked.

He couldn't know that for once, Gail's ability to put herself in another's shoes had failed her. She didn't even hear the last three words, only the ones that went before, and they fell on her heart like lead weights.

"Of course, we can," she said. "After all, nothing *did* happen, really."

The school holidays seemed to speed by, and suddenly it was the day before the children were to return to Kenleigh Grange. Everyone was in a subdued mood. Gail couldn't even distract herself by writing. The book had been finished and sent to the publisher, and now, when she wasn't trying to cheer Steve up, she was in torment for herself, certain that it was rubbish and would come winging back.

She began going for walks in the evening, partly to let Steve and the children have the house to themselves and partly because she needed to be alone. One evening she borrowed Steve's car and drove into the centre of Chalmley. She wandered around aimlessly on foot for a while before going into a small restaurant where she'd never been before.

As she was looking around, trying to decide where to sit, her eyes fell on a table by the window. It was occupied by a dark-haired young woman with a strong, attractive face, and a young man who was holding her hand and speaking with great intensity. After a moment Gail realised that the man was Harry.

She hadn't recognised him at first because his face bore an expression she'd never seen before, and it altered him like a disguise. Harry was deeply in love. Nothing else but love could have given him that look of anguished intensity. He was vulnerable as people were who discovered deep feelings for the first time, and Gail looked at him in wonder.

At that moment he looked up and saw her, and at once she could see he was nervous. Poor Harry. He didn't want his ex-fiancée causing problems with his new love. Gail gave him a reassuring smile and quietly went away.

On the last night, when the children had gone to bed, she and Steve sat together, trying to make plans for the future. "It'll be all right," she told him. "Judges ask children what they want these days, and Nell and Kevin want to be with you."

He sighed. "Let's hope you're right about the judge."

Before she could answer there was a knock at the French doors. They looked up and saw Lady Kenleigh standing there. "Oh, good grief!" Steve said furiously. He went to open the door. "We agreed they should come back tomorrow," he snapped. "They've gone to bed."

"Of course. I haven't come to disturb them. May I come in?"

When she was inside she looked directly at Gail, as if seeking her help, and suddenly Gail knew what was going to happen, knew it with total, thrilling certainty. Lady Kenleigh cleared her throat and addressed Steve. "I've come to ask you a very important question, Steven. Mrs.—your wife—told me recently that if I let the children go back to Boston with you, you would allow me to visit them when I wished. I should like to know if she spoke for you."

Steve looked at her for a long moment, then at Gail. "Yes," he said at last. "You can come whenever you like."

A slight shudder passed through her. She looked very old and tired suddenly. "In that case—I shall instruct my lawyer to tell the court that I no longer seek custody.''

For a moment Steve looked as if he hadn't quite understood her. Then he said, ''Do you mean that, Cornelia?''

''We've got to bring this to an end for their sake.''

''There's nothing I want more. But don't raise our hopes only to dash them again.''

''I wouldn't do that.'' She smiled wanly. ''You may not believe this, but I'm a woman of my word.''

''As a matter of fact, I *do* believe it,'' Steve said perfectly seriously. He touched her arm. ''We haven't always understood each other, but perhaps that will improve in the future, when you visit us.''

''I know they've gone to bed but—may I see them?''

''I'll get them,'' Gail said before Steve could speak. She wanted to get out of the room before her face gave her away. If she thought hard for a few minutes she was sure she could manage to feel nothing but happiness for the little reunited family.

She roused the children, telling them only that their grandmother was here. It was Lady Kenleigh's privilege to make the announcement. When they all went downstairs, she was smiling cheerfully.

Lady Kenleigh looked at her grandchildren with eyes that were suspiciously bright, but her voice was steady. ''Your father and I have been talking,'' she told them, ''and we feel it would be best if you went back to Boston to live with him.''

The children gave whoops of joy and flung themselves on their father. But then Nell asked, ''We *will* see Gran, though, won't we?''

''She'll come to visit us,'' Steve assured her.

''Lots?''

"Lots."

At the sight of his children's delight, Steve had an overwhelming sense of relief, like a man who'd only just seen the pit at his feet. He knew a passionate surge of gratitude towards Gail, who'd kept him from falling in. His feelings were still sore against Cornelia, but now he knew that he could control them, not to spoil his children's joy.

"Daddy," Kevin said, "when will we be going home?"

"I don't know. I suppose there'll be formalities—"

"I think Mr. Brace can arrange a hearing in a few days," Lady Kenleigh said.

"And after that there's nothing to stop you going," Gail added.

Nothing to stop him going away from her. And he'd counted on having so much time to teach her to love him. He sought her eyes, but she was looking at Lady Kenleigh, smiling encouragement. And suddenly the little time left seemed terribly short.

CHAPTER ELEVEN

LADY KENLEIGH was as good as her word. At the court hearing a few days later, Mr. Brace formally said that his client was now convinced that the children's best interests would be served by living with their father. This time Nell and Kevin were present, and the judge, the same one as last time, asked them if they were willing to live with Steve, and he seemed impressed by their eagerness to go with their father.

Lady Kenleigh sat with her head bowed while this was taking place. Sir William hadn't bothered to accompany her, and she was quite alone. Gail watched her with aching pity and respect for the courage that had enabled her to do this. Steve followed her gaze, but said nothing.

At last it was over. The judge formally ended the wardship of the court and declared Steve free to remove his children from Britain. Steve simply closed his eyes and clasped Gail's hand tightly.

Afterward he went over to Cornelia and put his arm around her shoulders. "You'll be over to see us in no time, won't she, kids?"

The children eagerly assented, and Gail watched them, smiling, thankful that Steve had found the way at last.

There were still several days to go while arrangements were made. Gail felt suspended in limbo. It might have been her imagination, but it seemed to her that

Steve was avoiding her eyes these days. But then, she was avoiding his.

She was so much in the habit of working late that even when the book was finished she lay awake until the small hours. One morning she slept late and was awakened by the sound of the telephone ringing. After waiting a few moments she realised that she was alone in the house and got out of bed. She staggered as her head swam suddenly and clutched the dressing table, trying to fight off the nausea that threatened to overwhelm her. At last she had it under control and managed to get downstairs to the phone. "Hello."

"Gail?"

She sank onto the window seat, her face brightened at the sound of Dan Protheroe's voice. He was her editor, a jovial man in late middle age, and his faith in her work had kept her going. She'd heard nothing from him since sending off *Drake Domino and the Evil Eye* to him. "I suppose it's too soon for a reaction?" she said hopefully.

"Too soon? I took it home the day it arrived and sat up all night to finish it. My wife kept saying 'put that light out,' and I kept saying 'just another few pages, dear,' until I'd got to the end. Congratulations, Gail. This is the book I knew you could write when I read the first one."

"You think it's better than the others?" she asked, although her own instincts had told her the answer.

"Streets ahead. The first two were marvellous, but they came from your head rather than your heart. You were far more involved this time. The really brilliant stroke was to bring Professor Savernake into the spotlight and make him the hero's equal. He's a wonderful character now, and he's the real reason I've got some good news for you.

"I showed your manuscript to a television producer, and he called back the next day asking to see the first two books. He wants to do a series of four hour-long plays. Both Domino and Savernake will be played by stars. We must have a conference soon about the fourth book, and you'll have to write it very fast. I can give you a much better advance this time because those TV shows will be sold all over the world, and so will the books. This is it, the big time at last. Gail—are you there?"

"Yes, I'm here."

"Aren't you delighted? I thought you'd be bubbling over."

How can I bubble over when my world is disintegrating? I can't even remember how thrilled about this I'd have been once.

But Dan was a kind man, and he'd worked hard for her, so Gail strove to put some enthusiasm into her voice as she thanked him. He talked on for another ten minutes, outlining her glittering prospects, and finished, saying, "We'll have lunch at the Ritz next week. Bring along lots of ideas."

The queasy feeling was there again. She hurried upstairs and returned to bed, taking deep breaths until the worst was past. She lay staring at the ceiling for an hour, occasionally laying a hand over her still-flat stomach, puzzling over the strange turns her life was taking. One heart's desire was gained and one would soon be lost, and the one she was losing was the one that really mattered. She could do without success. She could even, if she absolutely had to, do without writing. But she couldn't do without Steve. Yet Steve was going away, apparently indifferent.

Now there was a new complication. She'd had her suspicions for the last few days, but this nausea had confirmed them, and she didn't know what she was going to do. Should she tell Steve, whose paternal heart would make him invite her to stay with him for the sake of his child? Could that ever be enough for a woman who yearned for so much more?

At last she rose and dressed. She felt well again, and the colour had returned to her cheeks. It was strange to look so good while her heart was heavy. She made a mental note of it for future reference, but there was no flip of pleasure that the magpie storing of information usually gave her. For the first time it felt like a chore.

She heard the car draw up and looked out of the window to see Steve and the children pile out. Steve looked up and waved to her. Gail went downstairs to meet him. She'd made no decision except to be undecided. She must wait and learn from Steve's manner whether she should tell him her secret.

He came in and smiled as he saw her. "You're up at last. You were awake so long last night that I let you sleep. I've got something to give you." He rummaged in his desk and produced a sealed envelope, which he handed to her. "Open it," he said eagerly.

She tore open the envelope. Inside was a check for ten thousand pounds.

She stared at it in silence, trying to control the feeling of despair that swept over her. "But you don't owe me anything," she said at last.

"I owe you everything."

''But I was only to get another check if this went on for more than six months. It's been barely three.''

''I know but—please, Gail, think of this as a good-bye present.''

Nothing in her life had ever hurt so much. She loved Steve, and for a few weeks she'd known the happiness of being necessary to him. Once, she'd found rapture in his arms. Now, this was his idea of a goodbye present.

But you always knew it was a business deal, said the voice of common sense. *You can't blame him for treating it as one.*

''I can't take this, Steve. I didn't earn it, and I don't want it.''

His smile wavered a fraction before he said cheerfully, ''Nonsense, money's always useful.''

''But you don't know what's happened. Dan, my editor, called earlier.'' She briefly outlined the conversation, adding, ''So you see, I'm going to be a rich, successful woman, and it's all due to Professor Savernake. Dan says he's a fascinating villain with that extra 'something.'''

''Well, you've had a real-life villain around,'' he said lightly.

''That's true.'' They laughed together, both sounding slightly forced.

''But these riches will take time to come in,'' Steve pointed out. ''In the meantime you need money for somewhere to live. You can't stay on Cornelia's doorstep once I've gone. She'll know her suspicions were correct.''

''That hardly matters when you're safely away. But I shan't stay here anyway. I'm going back to my old flat.''

''That rabbit hutch?'' he asked, scandalised.

"I was fond of it, and it was really my own."

"You're determined not to take anything from me, aren't you?" he said after a short silence.

"Nothing I haven't earned."

"You won't even let me thank you."

"But you *have* thanked me. You helped me with my book. I'll be grateful for that all my days."

"Ah, yes, of course, the book. I was forgetting that that's all you care about. Well then, it looks as if we both gained exactly what we want. That's how it should be."

"Right."

He held up the check. "But I still wish you'd take this."

She pushed it back into his hand and managed to laugh. "Take your money and spend it on a good cause, like teaching that delinquent puppy to behave."

He grinned. "It'll take more than ten thousand pounds to do that. And that reminds me, I've discovered we can't fly home because Sammi's too young. Apparently she'd get dehydrated in the air. So we're going by boat."

"Good idea. I'll come to see you all off and then slip back here to my own home."

He thought of the little box where she would live without him, and the lovely house in Boston where he could have taken her if she'd shown the least willingness. But it was the shabby basement flat she called home.

"So it seems to be all fitting in well," he said. "Once Sammi's had her shots, we'll be off."

She was going to miss Sammi, too. In the few weeks they'd known each other, the mischievous pup had made her own place in Gail's heart, and the day before the departure she went into town and bought her two rubber balls as a parting gift. She waited until the others were upstairs attending to final details before going into the garden in search of Sammi. "They're to remember me by," she said. "I got two because you're bound to lose one."

Sammi looked up at her, head to one side, pleading for one last game. Gail romped with her for a few minutes, then picked her up and drew the warm little body against her. The puppy felt delicious, wriggling closer and thrusting her cold nose against Gail's neck. "Goodbye," she whispered, and felt the rasp of a small tongue.

There was a hard ache in her throat, and her eyes were blurred. She'd hidden her feelings for so long, but Sammi would betray no secrets, and Gail let the tears come, burying her face in the black fur.

Southampton would be a blur in her memory all her life. She went on board the ship and saw their cabins, and Steve busied himself with some details while she said goodbye to the children. They hadn't shown surprise that she wasn't coming with them, but Nell was looking at her with an odd questioning gaze. "I should be going now," Gail said at last.

"Scram, kids," Steve ordered quietly. When they'd vanished, he looked at her and said awkwardly, "What can I say?"

"Nothing. It all worked out wonderfully well for both of us."

"You really feel that?"

"We each have what we want, Steve."

There was a strange look on his face that she read as embarrassment. Suddenly she couldn't bear any more. There was a hard pain in her throat that would overwhelm her in a moment. "I hate long goodbyes," she said. "Let's make this a quick one."

"If that's what you want."

What I want is for you to take me in your arms and beg me to stay with you.

She held out her hand. "Drop me a line now and then to let me know how things go."

"Fine, I'll do that."

The call came for all visitors to go ashore. Steve walked with her to the gangplank. All around them people were hugging one another. She offered him her hand. "Bye."

"I'll never forget you, Gail."

"Nor I you." At the last moment she reached up and kissed him lightly, then turned and hurried down the gangplank, leaving him standing there.

He was still there, staring blindly at the shore, when Nell and Kevin appeared beside him. There were shouts, the sound of chains rattling, shouted goodbyes.

"I can see her," Kevin cried.

Steve followed his son's pointing finger to where a slim, blonde woman was standing in the crowd, waving to them. He waved back to her, then turned away abruptly.

In the week following Steve's departure, Gail was wined and dined by Dan Protheroe and Billy Jacobs, the television producer. During that lunch she had the eerie sensation that every crazy dream she'd ever dreamed of fame and success was coming true. She produced a rough synopsis of the next Drake Domino book, and they fell on it with delight. Dan demanded that she write it in two months flat, and she heard herself agreeing. Billy outlined the show he had in mind, and as she pictured it she knew that he'd understood what she was trying to do. The pleasure of falling in with a creative mind that was in tune with her own was so great that for the next two hours she almost forgot her sadness and enjoyed herself.

She floated home on a tide of euphoria. Her notebook was packed with ideas, and she couldn't wait to get started. She thought how foolish she'd been to forget that work conquered everything. She would have no time to brood.

But when she turned the key on her tiny flat and heard the silence within, something seemed to stop her heart. She couldn't endure to stay in the cottage where she'd lived with Steve and known a brief happiness. She'd fled to this place that had barely known him, thinking it would be a refuge. But now she seemed to see him sitting in the armchair as he'd done that day, flicking over the pages of the book. She closed her eyes in despair as her mood of hope drained away. Nothing had changed. Wherever she went, whatever she did, Steve would be with her.

She pictured him now, living with Nell and Kevin, their days full of joy at being together again. Then she gave herself a shake. It was useless to indulge in such thoughts, and she had work to do.

But how could she forget him when she carried the living reminder? It was early yet, but as the weeks passed she could feel herself blooming, growing a little rounder, and knew that the miracle inside her was greater than any pain.

She seemed to look at the world differently these days, seeing and understanding more. It was like becoming a new person, inside as well as out, and she was glad of it, for the change seemed to be bringing her the strength to cope with everything that was happening to her.

She'd had to fight for every word of the first three novels, but the new book seemed to flow out of her fingertips of its own accord. Now she'd found the key, everything was possible. She completed it within the deadline. Both Dan and Billy were loud in their approval, and Billy, who was doing his own scriptwriting, immediately began the adaptation. He sent her the first three scripts, and she was delighted to see that he'd caught the atmosphere exactly.

At Christmas there was a card from Boston. It featured a picture of Nell and Kevin sitting with Sammi, now grown out of recognition, except for the light of mischief in her eye. Inside Steve had written a few lines of well-wishing, such as he might have written to anyone. Gail wrote a cheerful letter back, talking about the television show that was expected to start rehearsing soon and the generous new contract for four more Drake Dominoes that Dan had given her.

When she read it through afterwards, the letter had a totally impersonal sound. For the children's sake she tried to find something warm to say, but she could think of nothing that wouldn't hint dangerously at her love and the continual ache of longing for Steve. At last she settled for, "My best love to Nell and Kevin," and signed her name.

The new year brought freezing temperatures, and she
stayed indoors as much as possible. But when her new
advance came through she invested in a small car and
enjoyed the independence it gave her.

On one cold day late in February she went out for
some shopping and decided to drop in at a small restaurant for a snack before going home. It was the one
where she'd seen Harry months before. It looked fairly
empty, and she went in thankfully. Then she saw that
Harry was there again, at the same table where he'd
been sitting with the young woman, but this time he was
alone, staring out of the window and drumming his
fingers. He looked up, saw her and smiled, patting the
chair beside him. She joined him, glad of the chance to
be friends again. His eyebrows rose as he saw her waist.
"Congratulations," he said. "I guess I owe you an
apology." He spoke naturally and without any self-
dramatising.

"What about?"

"Your marriage was real all the time. All that stuff I
said—" he shrugged "—I was out of line. I'm glad it
worked out for you, Gail."

He was different. His face was thinner and looked as
if he hadn't slept much recently, and all the bump-
tiousness seemed to have been knocked out of him.
"I've been reading about your television show in the
papers," he said. "It's wonderful that you made it at
last, Gail. I'm really glad for you."

"What about you?" she asked. "You don't look as
if things have worked out so well." He shrugged. "Are

you waiting for the woman I saw you with? I thought she looked nice.''

"Alice? Yes, she's very nice." He sounded sad. "By the way, thank you for leaving that night. It was kind."

"What's the matter, Harry? I've never seen you like this before."

"I've never *felt* like this before," he admitted. "I don't know where I'm going or what's going to happen next."

"Perhaps Alice can tell you," Gail said with a hint of mischief.

"Yes, perhaps," he agreed vaguely. "Let me get you some tea." He called a passing waiter, and when they were alone again Gail tried to lighten the atmosphere by saying, "Are you sure she won't be jealous if she turns up and finds you having tea with another woman?"

"I don't think there's any fear of that."

"She's not the jealous type? Lucky you."

"No, I mean I don't think she'll show up," he said simply.

Gail didn't ask him why he bothered to be here. She knew that painful, hard-dying hope. The only thing that surprised her was that Harry should know it.

Harry added, "We don't see so much of each other now."

"Her choice or yours?"

"Hers."

"But it didn't do this to you when I left," Gail said, wonderingly.

"No, well—" He became embarrassed. "That was different."

"Because it was only your pride that was wounded. But this time it's real, isn't it? You can tell me, Harry. We're old friends."

He shrugged. "Nothing much to tell. I met Alice soon after I came back from Brighton—"

"In this restaurant?"

"Yes, how did you know?"

"Just a guess. Go on."

"Well, I was knocked out." He played with a spoon, not looking at her as he said, "I didn't go cruising in the Aegean, after all."

"Because it would have meant being away from Alice?" Gail asked.

"Yes," he said, slightly red.

"Good for you."

"Everything was fine for a while, and then—oh, I don't know—she seemed to change."

"You mean you had rows?"

"No, she just became sort of elusive, making excuses not to see me. I know there's no one else. In a way it would be easier if there *was*. I'd know what to do. Or maybe I wouldn't. I tried it when you found someone else, and all I got was covered in ice cream."

They both laughed, but Harry's laughter faded almost at once, and he said desperately, "What is it that I do wrong, Gail?" Seeing her hesitation he added, "Give it to me straight."

"All right. Harry, this comes from a friend who wishes you nothing but happiness...."

"Well, that's prepared me for the worst," he said with a brave smile.

As gently as she could she said, "You're selfish, conceited and arrogant . . . or at least, you were. . . ."

"Before Alice knocked me for six? You tried to tell me when you left, didn't you?"

"Yes, but you couldn't hear me because I was the wrong person. But you really care what Alice thinks, don't you?" He nodded. "Then why don't you go and tell her?"

"I don't know how. Suppose she throws me out?"

"That's the chance you've got to be brave enough to take, Harry. Loving someone isn't easy. You can't offer your heart conditionally, because a gift with strings attached is useless. You have to give everything and risk getting nothing back."

"I guess so." He smiled at her. "You're the living proof that a gamble can sometimes pay off."

"Am I?"

"You've got it all, haven't you?"

Out of sight Gail laid her hand gently over her stomach where she could feel the swell of the baby. "I have a good deal," she said, smiling.

She stayed only a few minutes after that. If Alice should come in now and find Harry with her, it could be disastrous, and she didn't want to spoil things for him. She discovered that she liked Harry now a good deal better than she had when she'd fancied herself in love with him. "Goodbye," she said at last, rising. "I hope it all works out for you, Harry."

"If it doesn't, I'll know where to come for advice," he assured her.

Her car was parked a little way down the street. As she reached it she saw Alice appear around the corner and stopped to watch her. The young woman stood hesitating on the pavement for what seemed like an age, then she crossed the road quickly and went into the restaurant. Gail smiled, and drove home feeling almost happy.

CHAPTER TWELVE

THE last person Gail expected to see when she opened her front door was Lady Kenleigh. "May I come in?"

"Of course."

Lady Kenleigh stepped inside the poky flat and looked around her. Gail hastily pulled some papers out of the armchair. "I'll make some tea."

While she worked in the kitchen her thoughts seethed. It could do Steve no harm for Lady Kenleigh to know the truth at last, but it threatened her own secret. Her pregnancy was obvious now. Fiercely she castigated herself for not having the sense to move out of the district.

She returned to the living room to find Lady Kenleigh looking at the picture of the children with Sammi that Gail had had framed and kept on the mantelpiece. "Your career seems to be flourishing," the older woman remarked. "I've been reading about your television show in the papers. One of them mentioned you as living in Chalmley."

"And you came to see if it was true," Gail supplied. "How did you find me here?"

"Through your friends on the local paper." Cornelia sipped her tea delicately before saying, "So I was right."

"In your suspicions about our marriage? Yes. And I suppose you hate me now."

"I don't hate you. In some ways I'm grateful to you. You showed me what I was doing."

"Then why are you here?"

"Perhaps because I was curious. It's always nice to discover the end of the story." She met Gail's eyes. "But the story hasn't ended, after all."

"It has as far as Steve and I are concerned," Gail said. "We had an agreement, and we both kept our side of it. Without his help, my career wouldn't be flourishing."

"And that's all your marriage ever was? An agreement."

Gail was too tired to argue. "Yes," she said.

"Rubbish!"

Gail stared, taken aback as much by Lady Kenleigh's trenchant tone as by the word. "Absolute poppycock!" the woman went on. "Don't tell me that you aren't in love with him, because I shan't believe you."

"I—" Gail passed a hand over her eyes. "It doesn't matter now."

"Now that he's walked off and left you, you mean?"

"You talk as if Steve abandoned me," Gail said angrily, "but he didn't. I always knew he'd be going home when he had his children."

"But he doesn't have *all* his children, does he? Are you telling me he didn't want this one? It seems strangely unlike him."

"Lady Kenleigh—"

"It's nonsense for you to keep saying that," the other woman interrupted. "In future you'd better call me Cornelia."

It was more of a royal command than an invitation to friendship, and Gail took a deep, indignant breath before resuming, "Lad—Cornelia, I really don't think this is any of your concern."

"You mean the baby isn't his?"

Gail wished she could find some way to silence this inquisitive woman and order her out, but Cornelia Kenleigh had generations of command behind her. Gail found herself saying, "No, this is Steve's baby, but—"

"Of course, it is. I wouldn't have believed you if you'd said otherwise. Your child will be half brother or sister to my grandchildren, and that makes it very *much* my business."

Gail stared at her, baffled. "I'm beginning to understand how we won an empire," she said at last. "I'll bet there was a Kenleigh in every corner of the world telling the natives what to do for their own good."

To her surprise Cornelia gave a spontaneous laugh. "Certainly there was," she said.

The tension was fractured between them, and Gail found herself laughing unsteadily, too.

"Are you taking proper care of yourself?" Cornelia demanded.

"Yes, the doctor says I'm perfectly fit."

"Does Steven know about the baby?"

"Of course not. It was to be a without-strings arrangement."

"You'll forgive my saying so," Cornelia said drily, "but you appear not to have stuck to the terms."

"Things—got out of hand one night—"

"Things usually do when people are in love," Cornelia put in, more drily still.

"But we're not in love, at least . . . *he's* not."

"And so you let your pride get involved? I don't know about young people today. You none of you have any sense of responsibility."

"I beg your pardon?"

"What will it be like for my grandchild growing up with only one parent instead of a proper family?"

Gail forbore to point out again that her child wouldn't be a Kenleigh. This determined woman had just accorded it honorary status. Gail, who could be fairly determined, too, felt herself being simply submerged. Alarm made her speak peremptorily. "Cornelia, you've got to listen to me. I absolutely forbid you to tell Steve about this baby." Cornelia's eyebrows shot up but she didn't speak. "I know you mean well, but you really must not interfere."

Probably no one had forbidden Cornelia Kenleigh to do anything in the whole of her masterful life. "I see," she said, obviously at a loss for words.

Somewhat ashamed of the way she'd spoken, Gail went on in a milder tone, "Don't you see that if Steve only asked me to stay with him because of the baby, it wouldn't work? It would be useless. I should end up leaving him as Barbara did."

Cornelia gave a sigh. "You may be right. Very well, I won't tell him."

"You promise?"

"Of course. I'll be going over for a visit next week. Is there any message you'd like me to give them."

"Just my good wishes—and nothing about the baby."

"There was really no need to add that," Cornelia said, offended. "As I said once before, I'm a woman of my word."

She left soon afterward, still slightly glacial. To her surprise Gail found that the encounter had left her in brighter spirits. Over the new few days her mood varied. She was easily irritated by small things, but then her optimism would soar for no reason. She put it down to her advancing pregnancy.

She tried to keep her thoughts away from Boston, but they insisted on straying. Were Cornelia and Steve managing to get on better now? She had no fear of her secret being betrayed. A woman of Cornelia Kenleigh's mettle would go to the stake before breaking her word.

One evening a strange thing happened. The telephone rang and when she answered the caller hung up. This happened three times in an hour. ''That's all I need, a phantom caller.''

After the third time the telephone stayed silent, but the calls had contributed to her restlessness, and she couldn't go to bed. At two in the morning she was still sitting at the computer, when the doorbell rang. ''If this is another phantom . . .'' she muttered.

But the caller wasn't a phantom. It was Steve.

She stared at him swamped by joy, disbelief and bewilderment, and said the only words that would come into her head. ''You should be in Boston.''

''So should *you*,'' he said.

She stood back to let him into the apartment, her first thought that Cornelia had betrayed her. Then she saw Steve's eyes fixed on her waistline, and there was no mistaking the look in his eyes. It was sheer thunderstruck amazement. ''All this time—and you didn't tell me?'' he managed to say. ''You let me go away...do you think I'd have left you here if I'd known?''

''I knew you wouldn't. That's why I didn't tell you. I didn't want to be a sufferance, Steve.''

''A sufferance?'' He echoed the words in disbelief, then, as if realising that words were useless, he opened his arms, and she went into them as far as her belly would let her. Which wasn't far. But they managed.

"Is that what you believed?" he asked when he could speak again. "And I thought you could read anyone's heart. I thought you knew how I felt about you, but that you didn't want to know. I was watching and waiting for some sign, but you never gave it to me."

"I can't read your heart," she said urgently. "I never could. You'll have to tell me."

"I must have loved you almost from the start. I was so wild with jealousy about Harry. But then you showed me how clumsy I'd been with Barbara, and I was afraid of making the same mistakes again and driving you away. I thought I had time to win you, but suddenly there was no time, and you never gave an inch."

"Steve, why did you come here tonight?"

"Because of something Cornelia told me."

"About the baby? But she promised—"

"No, it was something else, something you said." He was watching her closely.

"I said I was in love with you," Gail remembered. "And that's true."

He took her face between his hands. "Let me hear you say it again."

"I love you, Steve," she whispered.

"Why couldn't we simply have admitted this to each other long ago?"

"There were too many shadows."

"I don't understand that."

"I'll tell you later." She smiled. "Nell would understand."

"I can see you and Nell ganging up on me in the future, and probably Cornelia, too."

Gail gave an unsteady laugh. "Fancy her doing this for us."

"Well, she did it in her own inimitable way. She said if I couldn't see that you'd been in love with me all along, I was a bigger fool than she'd taken me for."

"That sounds like her."

"Then she said if I had any sense I'd get on the next plane to England. So I did."

"You came back with Cornelia?"

"No, she's still over there. She and the kids are having a wonderful time together, so I left them to it."

"Oh, Steve, I'm so glad."

"Yes, we're a family now, thanks to you. At least— we *will* be a family when you're there."

"If you love me, I'll come anywhere," she said softly before his lips closed on hers.

Some time later he said, "I'd better call home."

"Speaking of calls..." Gail said, remembering.

"Yes, it was me," he admitted. "I called three times from the airport to say I was coming, but I lost my nerve every time you answered."

When he got through to Boston, he said, "Cornelia? Yes, everything's wonderful—but you left something out." Gail could just hear Cornelia's cheerful laugh. She couldn't catch what she said, but Steve grinned. "Have the kids gone to bed?" he asked. "Okay, don't wake them, but give them a message in the morning. Tell them Professor Savernake won this one."

When he'd hung up he said, "She's trying to decide what we're going to call the baby."

"Oh, is she?"

"Let her have her way. The only thing that matters is that it's *our* baby."

He put his arms around her, and she went into them joyfully. The shadows of morning had gone forever. The shadows of night would never touch them. Their love had come at last to its glorious zenith, and it would stay there, bathing them all their lives in its full constant light.

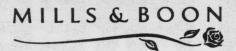

4 FREE

Romances and 2 FREE gifts just for you!

*You can enjoy all the
heartwarming emotion of true love for FREE!
Discover the heartbreak and happiness,
the emotion and the tenderness of the modern
relationships in Mills & Boon Romances.*

*We'll send you 4 Romances as a special offer
from Mills & Boon Reader Service,
along with the opportunity to have 6 captivating
new Romances delivered to your door each month.*

Claim your FREE books and gifts overleaf...

An irresistible offer
from Mills & Boon

Become a regular reader of Romances with Mills & Boon Reader Service and we'll welcome you with 4 books, a CUDDLY TEDDY and a special MYSTERY GIFT all absolutely FREE.

And then look forward to receiving 6 brand new Romances each month, delivered to your door hot off the presses, postage and packing FREE! Plus our free Newsletter featuring author news, competitions, special offers and much more.

This invitation comes with no strings attached. You may cancel or suspend your subscription at any time, and still keep your free books and gifts.

It's so easy. Send no money now. Simply fill in the coupon below and post it to -
Reader Service, FREEPOST, PO Box 236, Croydon, Surrey CR9 9EL.

- - - - - **NO STAMP REQUIRED** - - - - -

Free Books Coupon

Yes! Please rush me 4 FREE Romances and 2 FREE gifts! Please also reserve me a Reader Service subscription. If I decide to subscribe I can look forward to receiving 6 brand new Romances for just £10.80 each month, postage and packing FREE. If I decide not to subscribe I shall write to you within 10 days - I can keep the free books and gifts whatever I choose. I may cancel or suspend my subscription at any time. I am over 18 years of age.

Ms/Mrs/Miss/Mr _____ EP56R

Address _____

_____

Postcode _____ Signature _____

Offers closes 31st March 1994. The right is reserved to refuse an application and change the terms of this offer. This offer does not apply to Romance subscribers. One application per household. Overseas readers please write for details. Southern Africa write to Book Services International Ltd., Box 41654, Craighall, Transvaal 2024. You may be mailed with offers from other reputable companies as a result of this application. Please tick box if you would prefer not to receive such offers. ☐

mps
DIRECT MARKETING ASSOCIATION
MAILING PREFERENCE SERVICE

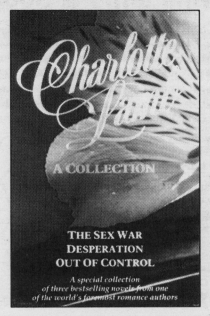

Next Month's Romances

Each month you can choose from a wide variety of romance with Mills & Boon. Below are the new titles to look out for next month, why not ask either Mills & Boon Reader Service or your Newsagent to reserve you a copy of the titles you want to buy — just tick the titles you would like and either post to Reader Service or take it to any Newsagent and ask them to order your books.

Please save me the following titles:	Please tick	√
A DIFFICULT MAN	Lindsay Armstrong	
MARRIAGE IN JEOPARDY	Miranda Lee	
TENDER ASSAULT	Anne Mather	
RETURN ENGAGEMENT	Carole Mortimer	
LEGACY OF SHAME	Diana Hamilton	
A PART OF HEAVEN	Jessica Marchant	
CALYPSO'S ISLAND	Rosalie Ash	
CATCH ME IF YOU CAN	Anne McAllister	
NO NEED FOR LOVE	Sandra Marton	
THE FABERGE CAT	Anne Weale	
AND THE BRIDE WORE BLACK	Helen Brooks	
LOVE IS THE ANSWER	Jennifer Taylor	
BITTER POSSESSION	Jenny Cartwright	
INSTANT FIRE	Liz Fielding	
THE BABY CONTRACT	Suzanne Carey	
NO TRESPASSING	Shannon Waverly	

If you would like to order these books in addition to your regular subscription from Mills & Boon Reader Service please send £1.80 per title to: Mills & Boon Reader Service, Freepost, P.O. Box 236, Croydon, Surrey, CR9 9EL, quote your Subscriber No:.................................... (If applicable) and complete the name and address details below. Alternatively, these books are available from many local Newsagents including W.H.Smith, J.Menzies, Martins and other paperback stockists from 8 October 1993.

Name:..

Address:...

....Post Code:........................

To Retailer: If you would like to stock M&B books please contact your regular book/magazine wholesaler for details.

You may be mailed with offers from other reputable companies as a result of this application. If you would rather not take advantage of these opportunities please tick box ☐

Steve Waugh's
SOUTH AFRICAN TOUR DIARY